, 1987

Monsieur Melville
VOLUME ONE

On the Eve of *Moby-Dick*

Monsieur Melville
by Victor-Lévy Beaulieu
VOLUME ONE

On the Eve of *Moby-Dick*

translated by
Ray Chamberlain

The Coach House Press · Toronto

Monsieur Melville was first published
as *Monsieur Melville* in 1978 by
VLB Éditeur, Montreal.

This translation copyright © 1984 Ray Chamberlain.

Coach House Quebec Translations are edited by
Barbara Godard and Frank Davey.

The translation and publication of this
edition have been assisted by grants from
the Canada Council and the Ontario Arts Council.

This translation was edited by Barbara Godard.

CANADIAN CATALOGUING IN PUBLICATION

Beaulieu, Victor-Lévy, 1945-
  Monsieur Melville

Translation of Monsieur Melville
  Bibliography: v.
  Includes indexes.
  Contents: v. 1. On the eve of Moby Dick –
  v. 2. When Moby Dick Blows –
  v. 3. After Moby Dick, or, The reign of poetry.

ISBN 0-88910-239-2 (v. 1).
ISBN 0-88910-241-4 (v. 2).
ISBN 0-88910-243-0 (v. 3).

1. Melville, Herman, 1819-1891.
2. Melville, Herman, 1819-1891, in fiction, drama, poetry, etc.
I. Title
PS2386.B4213 1984 813'.3 C85-098209-X

For Michel Garneau
since upon the steeds of our words
rides true friendship.

And for Guy Laflèche
for his generosity and his friendship –
because he read this work carefully
and without his precious advice
it would be less than it is.

Contents

CHAPTER ONE
In which the author dismisses his creatures to bring forth Monsieur Melville 11

CHAPTER TWO
The first images of Monsieur Melville:
As an aged man 23
As the creator carried away by the urgency of the work to be accomplished 31
As the father obsessed by his son Malcolm's suicide 32

CHAPTER THREE
Monsieur Melville apprehending his death 35
To lose all for one's writing 38

CHAPTER FOUR
Monsieur Melville's birth 43
Monsieur Melville's parents 44
Monsieur Melville's childhood 49
A question of language 50

CHAPTER FIVE
The world of Allan Melville, the father 63
America when Monsieur Melville was a child 63
The Melvilles' bankruptcy 68
The departure for Albany 75

CHAPTER SIX
The days following the move to Albany 79
What is reflected in all writing 82

CHAPTER SEVEN
The death of Monsieur Melville's father 87
Monsieur Melville and Gustave Flaubert:
to write because you cannot talk –
a fact of the utmost importance 88

CHAPTER EIGHT
Using childhood to get to the *how* of
Monsieur Melville 93
The choice of Augusta as Monsieur Melville's
privileged interlocutor 94
Monsieur Melville's adolescence:
the dream that takes place 97
At the State Bank in New York City 99
The spring of 1836: return to Albany 104
Monsieur Melville's decision: to throw himself
into the sea 106

CHAPTER NINE
To reach the end of Monsieur
Melville's adolescence 107
In which the author's creatures reappear to
turn the book into fiction 111

CHAPTER TEN
Monsieur Melville's maiden voyage – from New
York to Liverpool aboard the *Saint-Lawrence* 119
Sailors go round the world but
never once penetrate it 128
Redburn and Harry Bolton 129

CHAPTER ELEVEN
After the first voyage: just another idle hand   133
Monsieur Melville becomes a teacher in
the Sykes District   135
Signing on the whale ship *Acushnet*   141

CHAPTER TWELVE
In which the author dreams, full of desire   143
At the Melville Museum in Pittsfield   144
Meeting Monsieur Melville on the
docks of Harlem   147
With Lizzie and Melville in the
heart of New York   151
Monsieur Melville's and the author's stagecoach
ride and their arrival in New Bedford   155
Monsieur Melville, Queequeg and the author
meet in Peter Coffin's room   163
Nantucket as recounted by Monsieur Melville   167
Whale fishery thanks to Master
Henry Mitchell Havemeyer   173
  1. The myth of the whale   174
  2. The whaling industry   178
  3. The Québécois whale   182
In which Monsieur Melville forsakes
the author   189

> Jonah did the Almighty's bidding.
> And what was that, shipmates?
> To preach the Truth to the face of Falsehood!
>
> HERMAN MELVILLE, *Moby-Dick*

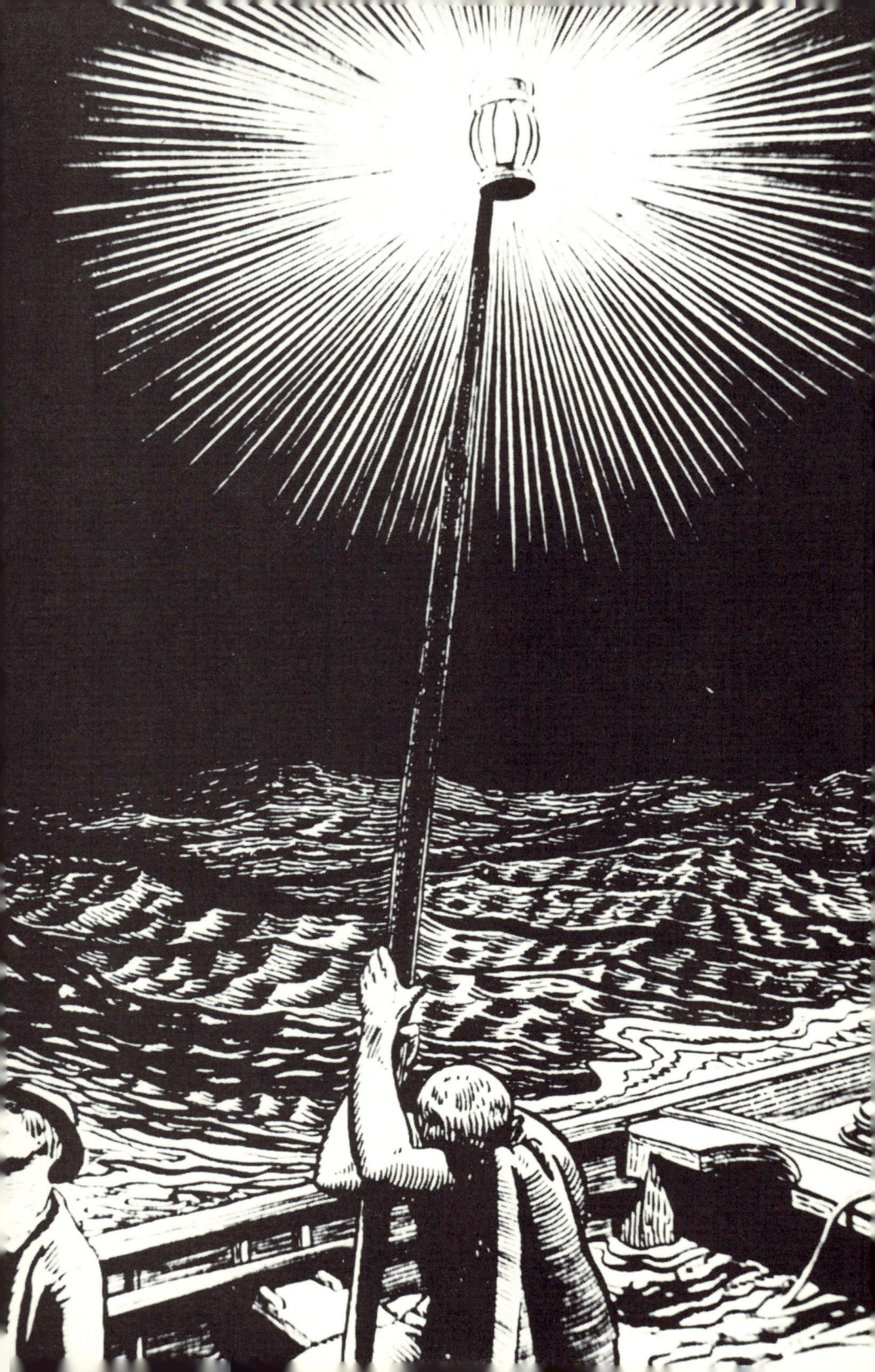

I

So, I had to bring them all together and let them know what I'd decided about them. I figured they weren't going to like it, but as far as I was concerned, I had no choice: I'd been stalling for two years, now ready, now undecided, my own coy mistress; engaged, in fact, in a veritable tug of war with myself, unable to get started – ranting and raving and never purged.

Because you're never better off than with a book you haven't yet begun: you let its savage life flow freely inside you, movement as sovereign as still-virginal passion, a searing madness owing nothing to anyone; the pleasure it provides is your only end – and that's when you have to get tough with yourself or else become mired in it.

By dint of living with the *other*, in the world of the other's words, you come to forget that world's power, you get so used to it you wind up silencing it, killing all the beauty which once nourished you. Haunting the book to be is this very exhaustion of the images garnered from the other, now so much a part of you they've become your own without you offering anything in return.

Still, I couldn't bring myself to do it. Days followed upon days and I pushed any thought of beginning ever deeper down inside me. I spent my time looking back, mentally leafing through the books I'd already done as though it had been possible to return to them and make them what now I wanted them to be. My mania wasn't due to some new novel but to that 'totalizing' idea of myself that I was looking for. Yet, rereading myself I became desperately aware that everything behind me was simply a collection of disconnected fragments, my poorest part, so to speak, little more than a residue – an aggregate of acts which I had fixed fast in words, but not well enough, because it was all still churning inside me, just as if none of it had ever been said. From those strings of words already set down came others, as well as from what had gone on within me since I had written them; so that I was left with the fact of their inadequacy – the fact that they would always be inadequate because of their past stretching into the future: it was difficult to accept because to some extent it meant facing my own negation, turning up the vulnerable underbelly of desire.

How to arrive through words at the best part of yourself, at what you sense deep down? At that beauty that is exclusively yours, that no one but you knows how to create? Rightly speaking, it's your whole life's justification – and much more besides, surely. How to describe, or inscribe it? With what words to call it forth?

There's no easy answer; the powers I invest myself with are so fleeting and unruly that none of what's behind me is ever any help; instead, it's a hindrance. Having failed so many times to produce beauty, how could I have hoped to capture it finally in a future work whose slow and painful stirrings were perhaps merely a way of forgetting what was so incomplete, so unsatisfying – to me, in particular – about the texts I had written? It was as though all I had said were merely a threshold, a perpetual possibility; a detour, too, no doubt.

There, more or less, is what I was tossing around in my mind when I asked them to the meeting. I had just finished a novel which throughout the moment of its writing had flowed from my fingers, so to speak, steadily and elusively, stealing to the farthest reaches of a space not mine but its own. I grew angry: it was such an easy, and at the same time, so traitorously impossible a task!

Because words point in too many directions. It grows burdensome. Because inventing a character isn't very difficult. To give him a certain number of traits – nothing superhuman in that, either. While constructing a plot is child's play at times. No, my problem definitely didn't stem from such trifles. Rather ridiculously, it came from elsewhere – from Job J Jobin, from that character whom I'd selected momentarily from among all the others, and about whom I was now able to say a great deal, impose on him all the words I wanted, any situation which by a few linguistic tricks I could render plausible, at least to myself. Once the last word was written, the novel would seem to be a unit; people would find a precise intention in it, a chronology and a particular time, as though the book couldn't be any different from what I'd made it.

While the truth is entirely otherwise: I chose *those* situations but could just as well have chosen any of an almost frightening number of others, even if they should contradict those I finally used in my book. So that even once the book was written, it remained unfinished in my eyes. Whence my anger and this idea that had taken hold of me, both provoked by the plurality of writing and its serial inscription – enough to damage any man's design.

Writing can't provide orientation because it doesn't begin and end, because it's pure rebeginning with an eye to filling in the cracks, while causing others, and still others, till one himself slips through to extinction. Of a house, at least you can say it's a house. But of a word, a series of sentences, an ensemble of texts, what could you say that would make any sense!

But there they were, all of them, together before me for the first time, forced to be there because I'd left them no choice; they had to come or go away forever. Some reacted violently, brandishing their fists the moment they arrived. I should add, though, that most were civil, something I hadn't expected. They were seated in various places around the large room, crossing and uncrossing their legs; their eyes were red. So many prominent paunches – God, what cruelty! I left them time to get acquainted and to feel their mutual complicity. It took a while for some of them to open up. Others had a hard time remembering in which novel I'd placed them. There was a brimming large punch bowl on the table in the middle of the room; Father was serving.

I had to address them at once so that it wouldn't drag on uselessly; also, so that my control over them shouldn't be weakened. Although I'd invented them, they belonged to me now only by virtue of certain trappings I'd draped them in which, though written down, had somehow stayed with me – meaning that one of these days, in some ill-advised work or other, I would have to pick up where I left off if I was ever to be rid of them for good.

Regardless, none of my characters made much of a fuss. All took note that I was sending them away for a while. My brother Steven compared me maliciously to a head doctor, then called me an Inquisitor who was over the hill, even adding that by my attitude it was as though I were signing each of them a letter under royal seal. The letter gave them liberty to do whatever they wished for two years without fear of repression from the part of me that ruled as writer.

When I asked my creatures what they thought they were likely to accomplish outside of me, they were extremely vague. Obviously, the only one who spoke of a definite project was my brother Steven: with Gabriella's help he intended to translate *Finnegans Wake*, a task that would certainly take him the next two years and more. Father, always affable, and never more so now that he'd been granted his retirement, assured me of his fidelity, even promising to round up all the documents for the book I was thinking of writing: *La Grande Tribu*, which he would no doubt narrate. Only France and Job J Jobin were reticent; they accused me of abandoning them before I'd finished with them. So as not to feel guilty, I said I'd stretch my own rule and allow them to interrupt me in my work occasionally. France was slightly pitiful, anyhow, stuck bolt upright in her wheelchair with

Saint Bowery's-without-his-Walls he came (secunding to the one one oneth of the propecies, *Amnis Limina Permanent*) upon the most unconsciously boggylooking stream he ever locked his eyes with. Out of the colliens it took a rise by daubing itself Ninon. It looked little and it smelt of brown and it thought in narrows and it talked showshallow. And as it rinn it dribbled like any lively purliteasy: *My, my, my! Me and me! Little down dream don't I love thee!*

And, I declare, what was there on the yonder bank of the stream that would be a river, parched on a limb of the olum, bolt downright, but the Gripes? And no doubt he was fit to be dried for why had he not been having the juice of his times?

His pips had been neatly all drowned on him; his polps were charging odours every older minute; he was quickly for getting the dresser's desdaign on the flyleaf of his frons; and he was quietly for giving the bailiff's distrain on to the bulkside of his *cul de Pompe*. In all his specious heavings, as be lived by Optimus Maximus, the Mookse had never seen his Dubville brooder-on-low so nigh to a pickle.

Adrian (that was the Mookse now's assumptinome) stuccstill phiz-à-phiz to the Gripes in an accessit of aurignacian. But Allmookse must to Moodend much as Allrouts, austereways or wastersways, in roaming run through Room. Hic sor a stone, singularly illud, and on hoc stone Seter satt huc sate which it filled quite poposterously and by acclammitation to its fullest justotoryum and whereopum with his unfallable encyclicling upom his alloilable, diupetriark of the wouest, and the athemyst-sprinkled pederect he always walked with, *Deusdedit*, cheek by jowel with his frisherman's blague, *Bellua Triumphanes*, his everyway addedto wallat's collectium, for yea longer he lieved yea broader he betaught of it, the fetter, the summe and the haul it cost, he looked the first and last micahlike laicness of Quartus the Fifth and Quintus the Sixth and Sixtus the Seventh giving allnight sitting to Lio the Faultyfindth.

— Good appetite us, sir Mookse! How do you do it? cheeped the Gripes in a wherry whiggy maudelenian woice and the jack-

A page from *Finnegans Wake*.

Anonymous. *Flowers and Fruit.*
(The National Gallery of Art, Washington, D.C.)

her left leg in a cast that we'd all made sure to sign, hoping it would perk her up a bit. Una, though, had the last word. She stated flatly, 'Your two years don't bother me. I can write my own stories.'

On that we parted; there were handshakes and kisses all around. Of course, my brother Jos would have none of it. He was furious because in my last novel I'd had him put away at Longue-Pointe. He held a grudge against me, would for a long time. He left with Steven, which reassured me. One day I would do something good with Jos. But it would take time, a dozen years or so at least. I hadn't got there yet.

So I helped Father straighten the house; then when things were back in place, I went to the kitchen to work. I've always written my books there on the old table of apple-tree wood, facing the reproduction I bought for my parents when I was sixteen – the most ordinary still-life imaginable, but Father accepted it as though it were a royal offering: the act represented much more, in fact, than simple filial love.

People tend to think that writers need a hideaway in order to be able to work, that they couldn't write otherwise. Legend has it that we then fill the place full of books and a number of bizarre accessories which give one real status. It's never been that way with me, however; I've always preferred a felt-tip pen to a typewriter, this simple apple-tree wood table to a desk. And regardless of the number of books elsewhere in Father's house, there are few enough here. I've always written from memory. Even this book on Melville I'm about to undertake – I'd like to write it from memory too, dispensing with file cards and notes and such gadgets. I don't know if the Melville of whom I've now begun to speak will make any sense, if he'll be believable and capable of being understood – in 1850 neither his life nor his work showed he was either! He was a lonely man, and because he was I became so fascinated by him that a little while ago I had to tell my own creatures not to count on me for two years and to act as though I weren't there.

Really, writing's a curious determination. I *am* that determination, however, my every act is a part of it. Becoming's other guises leave me indifferent. And now that I know that it's easy to write, and that once the first works have taken shape it's just a matter of getting on with it, I rebel. Because I can't find my truths there. It's difficult for me to say this any better or more clearly. It's obvious that writing a book about anyone other than oneself is a pretext. But we ourselves are pretexts. What is there to tell then? Where to stand so that *that* place would be the true one?

Simply to want to answer this question is to shed some light on the subject. For then I'm obliged to interrogate myself, and everything around me also, the society in which I live – mine only because I was born into it; it imposes the rules of the game; I'm myself through refusal – 'over my dead body'.

In my world (where I've gotten to in my world), there's little room for hope, in other words, for that idea we inherit which would have us high-stepping into the future. To tell the truth, I don't understand much about much! I'm so easily led by events; and if I seem to refuse accepted notions, it's because I can't easily forget that I myself might be one. I find it difficult to intervene with words – and I get the feeling that when I have, I haven't really, a part of me always begs off.

Perhaps that explains why, particularly at this moment, I feel such distress; why, though a writer in full possession of his powers, capable of summoning any image I wish, of refusing it, too, I should at the same time experience this nausea – it's as if what I'd always sought were of no help to me now that I possessed it sufficiently well to base my entire life upon it.

Writing isn't very difficult, especially when you're as I am and can absorb everything, the sublime and the ridiculous, the perverse and the trivial. What's hard to accept is that it doesn't go further and deeper. Questioning some of history's great books, reading one after another the *Iliad,* the

Aeneid, the *Divine Comedy, Don Quixote, Moby-Dick, Ulysses, The Death of Virgil, The Recognitions, Giles Goat Boy and Finnegans Wake* – these are the masterworks, I say as I read, the most accomplished in all of literature; what almost obscene heights of beauty they present, what truly totalitarian realms beyond interrogation's reach, self-sufficient, unanswerable. Which amounts to saying that it would be vain and pretentious to want to make them one's own. But I want nothing else; that's the level at which I've set my sights as a writer. My passion isn't literature; rather, it's this presumption that on occasion literature can become something entirely other than itself, the farthest outpost of mankind's experience, freedom's first venture.

And I probe into these lives, and I probe into these works, and I probe everywhere but don't succeed in turning the things I know into knowledge. Without it literature is devoid of meaning, however, for the rest is often just the artful exploitation of a few recipes, old favourites, turning the writer into a sorry scribe and society's most conservative element – he who makes do with mere reproduction. Writing as winding down; the phrase may very well be exact. While I am driven by the pursuit of that sublime difference that would abolish what's past and, in so doing, push me across the threshold to what I am.

But I have to admit that this project rests on nothing, nothing except my life which I want to force out into the open once and for all. Someone, I don't remember who, said that to write a great book it took a great deal of naïveté, faith that is. And there's the whole problem – because I tend to side with the infidels, having only gratuity, my own, to come forth with: meaning that I'm called Abel Beauchemin, that I live in Québec, in this small, equivocal country whose history presents a single face, that of the colonized, marked by absence, immobility. I'm no White Nigger, and I've no right to 'we' or 'I'. I can hardly say 'one', I can hardly handle my equivocality.

Thus straitened, I stand not knowing how – how in hell – I could get out of this fix unless by digging my solid tunnel ever deeper. My creatures don't play much of a role in it except as episodic sources of support I seek in history, as enticements to withdraw back inside my limits. In a confused age such as I live in, what is a Character? I'd be better off rejecting the whole notion; it would give me access to another sort of literature and permit me at long last to build a bridge to the ancients, who spurned the device as an offensive reductionism, apprehending what literature would become: a psychological hodgepodge telling little that's of value about man – his petty faults, his petty qualities, his petty misfortunes; in other words, what should be swept aside. In other words, things we should never again have to bother ourselves with.

In any case, that's the point I'm at as I begin this work on Melville, a book I've let linger a long time inside me, writing lengthy passages in my head only to let them fade away without daring to actually begin it. Because I was afraid the book would lack beauty. How different from what I felt when I was writing the Hugo and Kerouac books. Sometimes you cling to your weaknesses for dear life because they're proof that you really are what you think you are. You lean on them, take refuge in them as though they were the most solid thing about you.

But with Melville none of that holds. With Melville it could only be otherwise: what Melville was – that's what I would like to be. Maybe it will come to nothing in the end; maybe I'll meet a prodigious refusal from without, that most hopeless part of the act of writing.

This being said, perhaps it's easier to understand that in order to undertake this book for real, I had to send my creatures packing and close myself off in Father's house. I who am so little drawn to the cloister, to this very peculiar form of solitude which leaves you day in and day out alone with a large sheet of paper and no one but Melville to keep you company. While I know next to nothing about him because I'm convinced you can't tell another man's story. A biography can't say who Melville was. It's bound to be vague, never more so than when it appears to be clear.

Which is why Melville, like me, can't avoid being fictional. When I talk about him, or about Whitman or Nathaniel Hawthorne or Captain Cook, it will be important to keep this in mind. Maybe what I tell really happened, maybe the books I mention were really written; I'll never know for sure. Anyway, that's not what fascinates me. I don't want to make a character of Melville. I've done my research to try to figure out how it is that I'm caught up in this circular world when everything should be leading me to verticality, to other definitions of myself. Why I make so little headway in writing – and what became of a great exception called Herman Melville – there you have what I'm about.

I don't know yet what I'll find at the end; myself, perhaps, but a self far different from what I am at present; transformed at last and armed with what I need to write *La Grande Tribu* and whatever it might lead to.

2

Nevertheless, I can't just barge in on Melville; like it or not, I have to approach him in a roundabout manner due to photos I know of him showing Melville as a man past sixty with a long, bushy beard, a full head of short hair and a strong nose; and that right eye of his wide open while the left is dark and cloudy and almost shut.

The first, that is, the most tenacious image I have of Melville is that of an aged man. I don't say that of an 'old man'; it wouldn't be the same thing at all. Also, that of an aged man enveloped in an austerity which far surpasses simple arrogance. As though all had stopped, as though all had ground to a halt, the world's spectacle as well as one's own. I look at the photo and say to myself, 'This man is called Herman Melville. Let's suppose it really is Herman Melville.'

And I linger over it awhile as though I myself had ground to a halt, being in no hurry to move on and shatter this first image of him as an aged man, a man I suspect of being resigned to oblivion, a remark of Melville's that is often quoted when they look into his life to try to explain it. But I'm certain it doesn't mean very much. Because wherever Melville is – and I can't readily determine where – someplace where nothing remains of what he once was – that sort of consideration can't mean very much. Nothing more can happen now, memory itself is idle. You can turn into anything when you're this aged man. Escape yourself, so to speak. Because of this limitless place which is to be yours for good, a place defying all reference. It's formless and things move slowly there; things rarely connect; it lacks qualities; all's adrift as in space, free-floating in the neutrality of indifference.

It's thus that I first imagine my Melville, as someone whose words have gotten lost, as someone whose life has strayed. Will Melville really say soon that every death shows a marble pallor and that it's to forget this tiny thing that, noisy as crows, we enshroud it in grave words? Maybe not. But that doesn't stop me, at the beginning of my book, from dreaming that he does in order to catch my breath and find the *incipit* that will allow me to continue, or begin again, in fact. After all, it's simply a matter of speaking about Melville and of substituting myself for him throughout the book so as to finally get at the truth, his own.

Whence the importance I attach to the photograph which I sit staring at almost unhealthily in order to hold onto my first image of him.

At the time the photo was taken Melville was no doubt living in New York, earning his living at the Customs House. A job that must not have been worse than any other for Melville when you consider what he had become. Or so I allow myself to imagine. Just as I imagine him leaving his house in the morning to go down to the docks, tapping his cane on the cobblestones and rarely needing to return greetings because no one had time to waste in recognizing him. The briny air – and I reflect that Melville must have been thinking of all he'd written in that other, former life of his, and that it must have made large black spots dance before his eyes: we change so little, and what does change is soon just so much dry, brittle wood, no hope – the words, those black things which crowd onto the white page, those things that Melville wrote in his small house in Massachusetts with his sisters serving as copyists. With, on occasion, the sound of his wife Lizzie's skirts to break the monotony of writing as she climbed the stairs to bring him a cup of hot coffee. That head that might have been exploding, all those tiny, round words flowing onto the paper so long ago, long before New York and this job as

Herman Melville towards the end of his life.

The Brooklyn Bridge.
Currier and Ives lithograph.
(Library of Congress.)

Inspector of Customs – and I reflect again that it must have been those words which came back to Melville as he left home in the morning and heard the familiar sounds of the port: screeching pulleys, loud, sonorous voices – all his surroundings, in fact, must have reminded him achingly of everything he'd written up to then. A few lines from the beginning of *Moby-Dick*, such as:

> Whenever I find myself growing grim about the mouth; whenever it is a damp, drizzly November in my soul; whenever I find myself involuntarily pausing before coffin warehouses, and bringing up the rear of every funeral I meet; and especially whenever my hypos get such an upper hand of me, that it requires a strong moral principle to prevent me from deliberately stepping into the street, and methodically knocking people's hats off – then, I account it high time to get to sea as soon as I can. This is my substitute for pistol and ball.

I don't know why it should be these words, and precisely these, that come to mind as I imagine this aged man of a Melville strolling along the Harlem docks with his right eye wide open to take in the barrels and casks stacked upon the ships' decks and the arrow-like masts high over the water. Perhaps because his son Malcolm is on my mind – a single pistol shot three or four years before, a single shot to the temple; and nothing was left in the room, nothing of Malcolm which could be recognized as such, not even that part of Melville which he must have carried in him.

It all coincided with Hugo's death, a celebration that was to last for three full days and see millions of Frenchmen singing in the streets. Yet, Melville and Hugo knew nothing of each other. The one had written *Moby-Dick*, the other *Toilers of the Sea*, the nineteenth century's two great sea books. They meet in several places: Ahab is there in Gilliat; the white whale dives to the bottom of the ocean to become the mythical octopus, that monster of the deep that every man is hunting. With a single symbolic difference: Gilliat triumphs over the forces of evil while Ahab is drawn fatally to them and is almost pleased when they find each other. Because Melville and Hugo lived in two different worlds; to be sure of this, I need only think of them in old age: Melville, Inspector of Customs to put an end to writing once and for all, and Hugo's corpse, full of the century, exposed beneath the Arc de Triomphe – to be laid to rest mid flowers and hymns as throughout Paris they sing his songs – become life-giving, sovereign forces.

And I still see Melville stepping along the Harlem docks, although his work is satisfying, perhaps, only to his wife Lizzie, who thinks it's good medicine for Melville to keep busy after Malcolm's death. He lets her think so. He lets them think what they like. Because Melville knows in his heart that he's far too aged a man to pay any attention:

> Uppermost was the impression, that whatever swift, rushing thing I stood on was not so much bound to any haven ahead as rushing from all havens astern.

There you have what I wish to imagine first about Melville in his private Hades. So little is left of his life; so much memory remains, however, that what is beyond reach survives as a secret to deliver. Herman's books were incubi, claimed his wife Lizzie. Why not? Melville had done what he could, and found the pall soon laid upon him because he wasn't cut out for what is called a career in letters. Melville's writing shows no patience whatsoever, rather a stupendous assault on sainthood which when successful, as Jean-Paul Sartre has shown, is nothing more than a headlong dive into the asocial, a relentless exploitation of difference.

And there you have Melville's struggle, perhaps, age really having nothing to do with it. Yet I use this aged man as an *incipit* in order that the book might begin. I wish to know both the *why* and the *how* of Melville: what led him to accept the job as Inspector of Customs which placed him at one and

Peter Blume. *Eternal Life*. (Museum of Modern Art, New York.)

the same time within his dream of writing and forever beyond it – possibility become its own negation and leading to nothing but lifeless life throughout all those long years of old age – everything saying that this being, Melville, had undergone a metamorphosis?

After the collapse of his writing, the shock *Moby-Dick* was for him, I notice a change: henceforth, it isn't literature that's beyond reach and refuses to yield itself up but Melville himself within the shadows of his thorough, self-imposed resignation – thus giving rise to the paradox: why, in full possession of his powers, does he fall silent? Why does his style, so sovereign in *Moby-Dick*, falter suddenly and fail to move forward, sapping such work as follows of its powers of providing sustenance?

These questions are a part of this work because they constitute the knotty core of what first struck me about Melville, the great writer who lived the Great Failure.

I know I'll have to come rather far back now and undo the first image got from his photograph, since as I sit writing Melville is still on the docks of Harlem; he could walk up and down them for years because he no longer knows tiredness; though troubled in mind, perhaps, as he thinks, 'Poor Malcolm!'

All that blood for nothing; and that closeness to the son; that death because Melville wasn't, couldn't sire and nourish life.

I stop in spite of myself, the felt-tip pen falls from my hand. This overwhelming emotion that assails me the moment I think of Malcolm. To the point that I'm forced to chase the thought away. I think rather of the fact that they're soon to retire Melville. He'll be sixty-eight then, which means that he won't have much time – perhaps just enough before passing on – to speak of Malcolm: in that ultimate, stunning, guilt-ridden work which isn't to be published until after his death – *Billy Budd*.

Thus Melville's thoughts – as I imagine them from the

photograph – as he does his job as Inspector of Customs. That pain at the base of the skull from staring at too many barrels, all the crates full of clothes or bottles, with every manner of thing written upon them; coughed up by the sea and destined to disappear deep into the country – a glass of bourbon in Washington, a long flowery off-the-shoulder dress in Seattle, the glow of a Havana cigar in Boston. So much work! The outcome of so much work!

'They talk of the dignity of work', Melville writes. 'Bosh. True Work is the *necessity* of poor humanity's earthly condition. The dignity is in leisure. Besides, 99 hundredths of all the *work* done in the world is either foolish and unnecessary, or harmful and wicked. Whoever is not in the possession of leisure can hardly be said to possess independence.'

This was written to a female cousin. Melville knew whereof he spoke, he who in his life had never been able to do what he wished when he wished to do it. Not merely wishing but being possessed by the thing, it living in him, he living off it, swept up in its breath; lost, so to speak, and full of a sense of urgency about what was yet to be done.

Here you have my second image of Melville. To fill it out, give it depth: The writers whom I'm instinctively drawn to – perhaps because I project myself into their all-encompassing, total undertaking – share Melville's sense of urgency. Even Virgil, in whom it appears in reverse. Why didn't he want to finish the *Aeneid*? Torturing himself over it, almost undone by it, setting about it, backing off, growing more feverish as the thing took shape; a truly exemplary effort at retreating from the task which left him not knowing which way to turn. And wasn't Joyce responding to the same sombre anguish when, fearing blindness, he searched desperately for someone who could continue his work, a writer like himself – with the same initials, who was born the same day, the same hour as he in that magical Dublin where Anna Livia Plurabelle lived? And Victor Hugo, who forced his family to shut him up in his study and stash his clothes in a closet under lock and key so he could exist solely within the singular space of the book he was writing?

They were all like Melville furiously writing *Moby-Dick* in less than a year, rushing towards the final sentence, becoming neurasthenic at the thought of not having enough time – the same as Jean-Paul Sartre, who stuffed himself with amphetamines to speed up his writing so that he could say it all in the quickest and most definitive way possible, as though writing were a frantic race against the clock, a race you know to be lost in advance but which you can't halt.

Those great upheavals in the body which kept Melville at his table working on *Moby-Dick,* rendered almost senseless by the purity, by the words, that is, that came too fast for his pen; out of breath, fearing exhaustion, he followed them, hoping only to last until it was finished.

This is what fascinates me, that phenomenal state, that crisis whose *dénouement* – or the impossibility of a *dénouement* – was to determine an entire life. At thirty-seven, Melville lived through the break that changed him as a writer to such an extent that the rest of his career, except for *Billy Budd*, reflects the sovereignty of his refusal.

After *Moby-Dick* the only kind of writing possible for Melville was an obstinate 'no', yet too magnificently calm to be merely a 'no'. This becomes apparent as you read *Billy Budd* – and perhaps I'll attempt to demonstrate that this small work uses a single metaphor to present its sole subject – the impotence of paternity. There the Character is none other than Malcolm.

And here is my third image of Melville, whom I imagine returned home from work, alone in his small study leaning over his indecipherable script writing this:

'It is Malcolm of whom I would like to speak. That pistol ball and that blood and what there was of Malcolm before. Which I silence in me even as I speak of it to myself, because it is difficult. My eyes, Malcolm had these very eyes, these same bags hanging beneath them. When he was running

Whale's tooth scrimshaw.

about Arrowhead and his aunts – but I'm hoary with age now, condemned to wander forever through it all, unable to truly touch it because it no longer belongs to me, and because I am not sure in my exacting solitude where I am returning from: to think that beyond life lies only more life, a subtle network without real purpose or place. No need to seek. All is fullness flowing like honey. In any case, one should not have to ask oneself so many questions. All those which *Moby-Dick* brought in its wake, all those come from elsewhere! The world is such a tiny place!

'I had just completed *Billy Budd*; I knew I would write nothing afterwards, after that silence within silence; for a final time I laid my pen upon the table, I rubbed my eyes with my thumbs and breathed a last great sigh of relief; I didn't need to know what I had just written. Nor did Lizzie. I would have liked to thank her because she no longer questioned me and had let me lock myself up ritualistically night after night in this room to write my small book. Even if I don't finally speak of Malcolm, it's as if I had. Malcolm is in it. He is in it because there comes a time when things jam, a curious centrifugal force keeps us from then on in the present; all is seemingly actual there inside the circle of oneself with what once was, and still is – memory irrelevant to the unrestrained, welling radiance of this perpetual epiphany. It's sufficient to die for that to happen. There, I think that I have said just about everything.'

3

Of course, the meaning of all this can't be very clear as yet. To make it so, I'll have to silence these fervent first images of Melville, centred on *Billy Budd* now, that final work provoking so many questions. How was Melville when he finished *Billy Budd*? Overwrought? Depleted?

It was just before his death which came on September 28, 1891, after several weeks of dizzy spells. Confined to his bed, alone, looking, perhaps, at what is left of walls when your sight has failed, not even trying now to convince himself that he was Ishmael saved from the white whale's waters by his companion Queequeg's casket-life buoy; he still had a short way to go but was unburdened at last of his guilt, his beliefs and his talents – merely Monsieur Melville awaiting death, Everyman's ordinary death into which he went that September 28, 1891, with his eyes closed and his hand resting on the manuscript of *Billy Budd*. Those odours of geraniums and roses in the large pots in front of the window. And Melville soon to die without his small glasses to recognize Lizzie, who remained at his side gently wiping sweat from his large brow with her fingers.

Lizzie's perfume, that perfume which made Melville sneeze when they were living at Arrowhead.

Dying in such circumstances must not be very difficult. Merely a matter, perhaps, of a mirror, some simple lines traced upon it, the shattering of the whole. Because the truth is elsewhere; it can't be in this September 28, 1891, for Melville was dead long before. It was Lizzie, I believe, who said as Melville lay dying, 'I think his brow to be full of a prairie-like placidity, born of a speculative indifference as to death.'

Given what, even at this point, I know of Melville, it couldn't have been otherwise: he'd been resting for twenty years in the neutrality of the body.

'But I'm not so certain,' Melville says. 'It's all going too fast and I'm becoming strangely slow as if I were being assailed, as though invested with the whole of experience. Since my real death, all's astir like a string of words in which I let myself be caught up and carried away. September 28, 1891, is indeed when that individual Melville took leave of me, and now and forever it is the life of others that will come to greet me in the complexity of images. So much water! And Malcolm! And all of us locked up in the secret each is for himself!'

Upon Melville's death, a well-known journalist wrote in the *New York Times*: 'This week a man of advanced age died

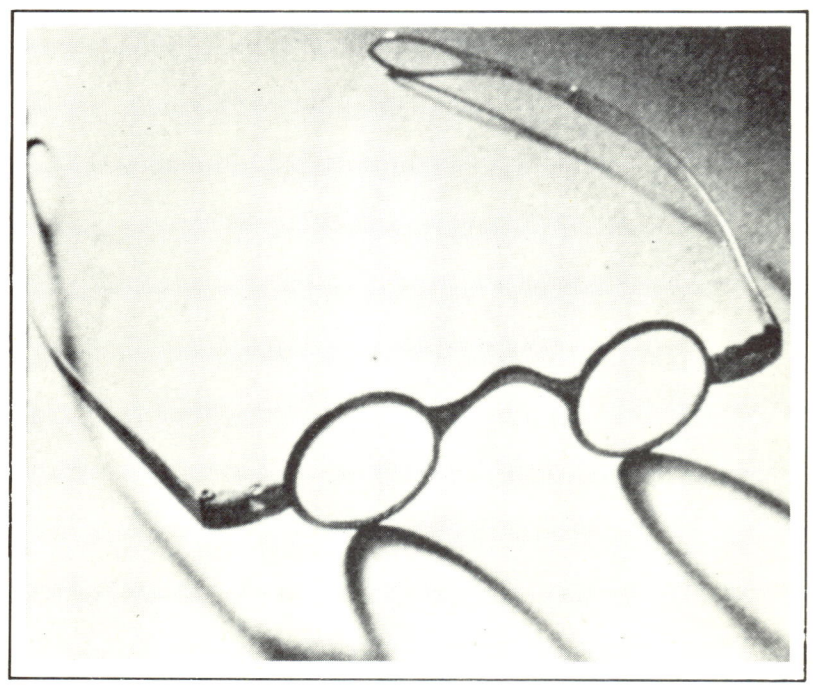

and was buried in this city, a man so little known, even by name, to present generations that a single newspaper printed his obituary, and the notice contained a mere three or four lines.' Nothing more – a mean fate. Which should give you some notion of what I am attempting in this book – a book that is really writing itself, heading I don't know where down the labyrinth of my questioning with the patient slowness that is mine now that I'm temporarily free of my characters and staying in Father's house. No need to seek reasons for my not beginning this book before today, other than this one: it requires a special place to write certain things, a place which makes them possible. Melville wouldn't have written *Moby-Dick* if he hadn't bought that small farm at Pittsfield and met Nathaniel Hawthorne. Without Pittsfield it would have died unformed within him.

And I need this old apple-tree wood table, and the small bouquet of dried flowers Mother placed on it a week before she died which, as though to show our fidelity, no one has touched since. All these things that greet one familiarly. I deprived myself of them deliberately for ten years because I was too involved in my various navigations to allow myself to think about them. I thought only of the work I wanted to do. That work took all of my time; I felt threatened by it, more so with each book I finished: my very organism was sinking as though it were being swallowed whole by my fury; the more I wrote, the more I was cancelling myself out, becoming less and less able to provide depth to my life. A surface – I was a mere surface with hardly enough space to exist in.

I mean – I wasn't living, it was my characters inside me who refused to die. Thus they drove me into a life that wasn't my own, indeed one that denied the very things I might have pretended to be. For a time I lost everything to the writer in me. Judith left me. She's happy now in that town in Florida raising the two sons Julien gave her, and happy for me because I've come back to Father's house after all those months of agonizing madness doing nothing but writing

around numerous bouts of bag-packing and the women I was leaving.

I've never understood very well the space between the imaginary and the real, since the latter has always seemed to me to be merely the activation of the former. But the weeks preceding my return to Father's house were truly insane ones. I who never drank was beginning to resemble the creatures I'd fashioned! I was guzzling forty ounces of Geneva gin daily and was unable to work in the mornings as before when I rose at daybreak to write a dozen full pages which then allowed me to do other things without feeling remorse or guilt. If it hadn't been for Father I don't know what would have happened. I was so full of Melville that it would have ended right there in the impossibility of writing anything at all, perhaps. At that time I didn't see the life our reunion would bring. At that time I couldn't make the connection between Father, my return to the family hearth, the sacking of my creatures and this book about Melville which I'd let linger inside me to empty it of passion, retaining only the reverse side, that is, his death which occurred September 28, 1891, after several weeks of dizzy spells – which could never be spoken, which would blame itself for failing to find its voice in me.

Sometimes when I'm writing, Father comes and sits in the chair at the other end of the table. He watches me. Or else picks up a book and flips through it, stopping at passages I've underlined, and trying to decipher the half-sentences scribbled in the margins. He remains silent throughout. Father can go for hours like that without moving for fear of disturbing me. He's a tall, thin man whose eyes have almost disappeared behind his thick glasses; in retirement he's growing a beard. I don't know why but to me it makes him transparent.

He spent the entire night with me thus. I wanted to begin my book at last. At the other end of the table I could see Father straining with me, looking for the right sentence. I

Anonymous. *The Kingdom of Peace*. About 1839.

was pondering Melville, my mind not yet completely free of the characters I'd sent away.

But perhaps it wasn't such a bad thing for the book to begin in this halting and roundabout manner. There was all that reading I'd done on America at the beginning of the nineteenth century; it had short-circuited me, so to speak, weighing me down with information, events and emotions; it made it difficult to get to Melville.

Regardless of the result, I had to begin at the simplest level. I thought of all the biographies I'd read, and I began to write what follows while Father emptied the sack of Maxwell House into the pot.

4

At the point I've reached, hardly familiar as yet with the odours of the old paternal hearth, Melville hasn't got very far. Because he's just out of his mother's womb, his navel still damp. We're in New York City, August 1, 1819. Together with Melville's first cries you can hear the clopping of the horses on the cobblestones outside on Pearl Street. In the house people are coming and going, excited by this pre-dawn arrival – a large baby whom his mother, Maria Melville, is holding in her arms. Standing next to the bed is his father, Allan Melville, his face flushed with emotion. He's a tall, swarthy young man who is proud of his curly side-whiskers, his dark, full head of hair and his large forehead which is common to all the Melvilles. The Gansevoorts, Maria's people, are a different sort: they have thick features and a strong nose, turning to aquiline in some, and thin lips.

'Gansevoort' has a nice ring to it. Because it's an old pioneer name. All the Hudson knew the name because the Gansevoorts had come to America at the beginning; they were as natural to this coast as its countryside, embodying the spirit of the North which in 1780 made Grandfather Gansevoort the celebrated hero of Fort Stanwix. In New York City, a street, a market and a hotel were named after him, and near Saratoga is Gansevoort Village, sacred repository of Gilbert Stuart's portrait of him: erect and wearing a wig à la Washington, in his Revolutionary general's uniform he looks a true swashbuckler, as Pierre Frédérick remarks, with eyes that run you through. His is a fine head, pure Gansevoort from the Dutch New York aristocracy of which the family was so prominent a part.

Though not as rich, the Melvilles weren't just anybody, either. Herman's paternal grandfather, Major Thomas Melville, won fame at the Boston Tea Party where he heaped crates of English leaves heartily over the side, shouting 'no taxation without representation!' But notice the coincidence: Boston in the place of New York, Major Thomas Melville finished up too in a Customs House. He finally lost his post under Andrew Jackson when America began its great westward expansion and upstart classes began to dislodge the aristocrats in place.

By the year of Melville's birth, the glorious past was quickly dying off, becoming a memory unto itself, the memory of old Scotland when one was a baron and seated at the right hand of Power. In a generation, nothing would be left of it.

Unlike the Gansevoorts, who had better resources, the Melvilles fell by the wayside; there was no place for them in an economy that was growing by leaps and bounds. When Jackson became President the old world caved in at last. Jackson's first swipe at it was his refusal to pay a visit to his predecessor – mannerless America's time had come, the men from the prairies were in the saddle, stampeding into Washington where they brutally shoved aside the men from the coast the country was born upon. Savage America was springing to life – the boom, rampant colonization, the Midwest. The old frontiers were falling and open spaces were creating the new man – that determined American who wanted to have everything and to be everything, caressing fame and fortune, caressing God and country.

In 1819 the Melvilles weren't yet able to imagine that they might be swept aside thus. Herman Melville's father: a rich man's son, himself a good bourgeois and walking among the family remembrances of revolutionary America; and less than anyone else able to understand the coming explosion.

Portrait of Melville's maternal grandfather by Gilbert Stuart.

Major Thomas Melville, paternal grandfath[er]

He was a well-heeled merchant who had grown up in easy circumstances. Before marrying Maria Gansevoort he took a long trip to France which perhaps gave him the idea to become an importer. Nothing could be more normal: after the generation of heroes comes that of merchants; how could Allan Melville have been an exception to the rule, living the outdated dreams of pioneers whose seats were cushioned with memories, living within the protective aura of the heroes of the Boston Tea Party and Fort Stanwix?

Sure, Allan Melville had travelled widely. Sure, Allan Melville was a handsome man. Sure, before marrying Maria Gansevoort, Allan Melville had nothing against the pleasures of *amour*. But that isn't what I seek in him. I seek what will lead me to Herman. And I find it in a detail; nothing really, an inoffensive mania of Allan Melville's. But a mania which tells me more than all the pages his biographers devote to him. It is that Allan Melville scrupulously noted the distances he travelled in a small notebook which he treasured. Why did he really have to know that he'd spent 643 days at sea and that his sea voyages amounted to 48,640 miles? Why did he really have to know that his trips overland amounted to no fewer than 24,425 miles? For the moment, I don't know. When Allan Melville goes bankrupt I'll have some clearer ideas about it.

As for the rest, found in any biography of Melville, I retain only the fact that Herman had seven brothers and sisters. He was the third child. Before him there was Gansevoort who was born in 1816. The next year brought Helen Maria. In 1821 came Augusta, and in 1823 Allan, Jr. In 1825 and 1827 two more daughters were born: Kate and Fanny. The youngest son, Thomas Melville IV, was born during the Jacksonian uproar which marked the beginning of the end for the Melvilles.

Right away bringing to mind this fact: Melville's universe was dominated emotionally by his mother and his sisters; his brothers counted for nothing. The women were by his side until the end, making his home their own. Yet they are nowhere to be found in his work aside from *Pierre or the Ambiguities* – how curious to discover that Melville, breaking with a long novelistic tradition, speaks entirely about himself, choosing his characters with care but never hiding from them, as he clearly states in *The Confidence Man*. Melville uses language in such a way that regardless of what he's saying, it's always about himself. In terms of nineteenth-century fiction, his is a peculiar stance: you are brought face to face with Monsieur The Author himself. Already in Melville's magical use of the 'I' one has strayed quite far from the long-established literary convention which held that the narrator, however present in the work, must never show himself.

In Melville the break with this tradition couldn't be more complete – and by putting himself as both character and author at the centre of the work, he gave the word 'fiction' its full meaning. For Melville the point was not merely to tell one story after another but to be involved in them at all levels of one's being. For Melville, writing had to be a total overcoming which at once absorbed and moved beyond one through the elimination of the phony division between the real and the imaginary. Whence the fury with which he writes up to and including *Moby-Dick*: he is searching not for the Character but for himself, he aspires not to motion but to its opposite – to say everything in a definitive book, everything about oneself and all else in one last book, that was Melville's undertaking. All was consumed in the fiery desperation of this search, painful to contemplate, there at the desert heart of impossibility. Long before it happens, I feel the need to report it from within Melville's soothing childhood – a childhood which, except for a bout of protracted illness, resembles everyone else's.

We know what transpires: things approach you, forcing themselves upon you, obliging you to figure them out and thus widening your range of sensibility. Storytellers are right to make the trees and the sun walk and talk: growth begins from without; the stuff of your surroundings becomes your meaning, your sense, by entering you and providing you with language. This common experience is the source of all orientation.

In Melville's childhood something more is involved, however. His biographers noticed it but saw nothing in it apparently, while I see there the explanation of the man's singularity. The father describes it thus:

> Herman is very backward in speech and somewhat slow in comprehension, but you will find him as far as he understands men and things both solid and profound, and of a docile and amiable disposition.

Some years later Allan Melville returned to the subject to add:

> Herman I think is making more progress than formerly, and without being a bright Scholar, he maintains a respectable standing, and would proceed further if he could be induced to study more – being a most amiable and innocent child.

The father's own testimony: as a child Herman Melville had difficulty with speech and language, he couldn't express himself, the words wouldn't come, nor that which holds them together. Words arrived from without and Melville couldn't interiorize them, make them material. That this should be at a time when things are forming and unforming inside one provides a hint that is confirmed when you've read his books – does this not give us the *how* of Melville when twenty years later he begins to write? I'll find further on that his real discovery of language – in the form of the utmost exploitation of metaphor – occurs in the period between *Omoo* and *Moby-Dick*. Since it results in failure, final, definitive failure, he reacts in a way which has baffled his readers: he writes that exceptional work *Pierre* whose pivot is his family, whose deep questions are addressed to it. As curious as it may seem, the work should have been his first because it poses the preliminary questions. Ordinarily a writer would proceed by writing *Pierre* first, *Moby-Dick* after. Why is it the opposite with Melville? What was so secret in the matter that it should be brought to the fore so late?

I reflect upon my own childhood and try to come up with the correspondence or coincidence that would permit me to make the connection. When Father was still calling me Bouscotte, I also had trouble speaking. For example, until Father gave me a good sound slap I kept saying 'Immaculate Consumption' for 'Immaculate Conception'. And even today I have trouble keeping my B's and F's apart. I almost always confuse them, just as I get mixed up when somebody refers to the left or the right, taking the one for the other.

Allan Melville.

Maria Melville.

Likewise, I couldn't understand why I was being forced to write with my right hand when I was left-handed; much less why they rapped me on the knuckles with a ruler to encourage me in it. All I know is that I hated to go to school, and I was convinced that as soon as I arrived the teacher would take her thick ruler out of her desk drawer. All day long the whole thing haunted me. So I pretended to write with my right hand when she was close by but the minute she turned her back I used my left. I didn't believe what the teacher had told me which, as far as I can remember, went like this:

> And above all don't be so foolish as to write with your left hand when nobody's looking! Your pencil will burn your fingers!

I'd tried it several times: I would hold the pencil for five minutes in my right hand then for the same length of time in my left. Up to a point the teacher was right – it was *hotter* in my left hand. But it wasn't unbearable so I persisted in what, because she didn't understand it, she called 'a nasty habit'. I listened in silence to the recriminations, and, contrary to my classmates, didn't try to take my hand away when the teacher struck me. Deep down I no doubt desired to write with my right hand. But I couldn't: in my right hand the pencil lost language itself; on the page there would be only indecipherable splotches.

I don't know what would have happened if Father hadn't persuaded the teacher to let me write with my left hand. What I do know is that I was aware of being unlike the others. It was brought home to me when she yanked me up from my desk and put me at the back of the classroom in the very last row. Of course, I couldn't understand this difference they were imposing on me. I understood only that because I persisted in that difference, in what was a way of recognizing who I was, I was cut off from the others, symbolically at least. Just as at home when I was made to sit at the foot of the table so as not to bump elbows with my brothers and sisters. In games it was the same thing: I'd never be good at baseball because apparently all of the gloves were made for right-handers. It was easy for me to think I was strange – wasn't all the difference in your hand?

This was a painful thing to learn because the difference between me and my school mates meant I would be less by just that much, by what, though forbidden to me, seemed to come so easy to them – beautiful handwriting, neat self-contained words which the teacher would show me to prove to me once and for all how wrong I was in my stubbornness, claiming with such conviction that it would bring about my ruin.

But though I forced myself to try again and again, it was hopeless: *I would never be able to write well.* What kind of man would I be? Because the problem had turned into something general, something absolute: everything came from the hand, I thought, language made its home in the hand. When you spoke, the words travelled up your arm and neck and came out of your mouth. Since mine came from the wrong side they couldn't be clear or nice to hear. That explained why I said 'Immaculate Consumption' instead of 'Immaculate Conception', 'vêtige' instead of 'bêtise' and 'Bonsieur' instead of 'Monsieur'. My left hand meant I was lost to real language; it showed in the songs I made up, nonsense syllables that made Father angry with me all over again.

Much later when I came down with polio – in my left hand, arm, and shoulder – I tried once again to write with my right hand, believing the other to be finished. I regarded it less as a catastrophe than as the end of my inferiority.

It was to be several years more before I made peace with my left hand. Before that could happen Bouscotte had to become Abel Beauchemin, novelist, whom I now remind to think about Melville's world instead – that ship without masts or sails adrift upon the high seas of great surging words.

54

Bouscotte.

Gustave Flaubert

I don't know why I'm writing this. Probably because Father has just sat down again at the far end of the table after serving me a coffee – *he's holding me by the hand, I'm going to school for the first time and I don't want to go. The train passes between the river and the road. All that smoke! Papa, I want to go back home. Please, take me home!*

I take a sip of coffee to help me get back to Melville. It's hard to see clearly into this famous question of language. Nowhere in anything Melville wrote nor in anything written about him do I find a clue to give the father's words their full meaning. Melville grew up in privileged circumstances: the large family house, aunts and uncles nearby, gargantuan meals – beautiful pieces of meat and succulent desserts – and devoted servants. How then are his difficulty with speaking and his slowness in learning in general to be explained?

In *L'Idiot de la famille* Jean-Paul Sartre hangs the whole problem of Flaubert on this statement: 'At nine Gustave decided to write because at seven he could not read.' Sartre proves this in a demonstration of more than three thousand pages – what I call the total book, one which begins with you and makes you the centre of the world, the prime mover setting all else in motion, achieving globality and inscribing it on searing pages studded with the black beauty of reflection. I can't avoid picking it up here and considering certain parts of it because I feel that the same facts account for both Melville and Flaubert.

Both came from a petit bourgeois world in which the family was omnipresent. The two fathers were alike in many respects: they both thought highly of themselves; they defended liberalism because it was their life; and they stood upon the shoulders of ancestors to whom they owed their place in society. But as Sartre saw so well in the case of Flaubert's father, it was all a flimsy façade:

> Achille-Cléophas would throw terrible fits which sometimes ended, out of sight of others, in tears; his nervous unbalance and mental tension were the result of his inadaptability:

despite being a successful doctor and teacher, or rather because he was, he had to struggle to remain integrated in that liberal society whose ideas he reflected but whose manners and ways upset him highly.

What strikes me most in Sartre's analysis of Flaubert *père* are the phrases 'nervous unbalance' and 'mental tension'. Because both may be easily applied to Herman Melville's father. His numerous voyages and his long stay in France show instability inherited from his ancestors, from the grandfather Thomas Melville notably, whom a biographer describes as 'slightly unstable, capricious and off-center' – particularly towards the end of his life when he walked the streets of Boston dressed in knee-breeches and a tri-cornered hat of the type worn in his childhood.

But Major Thomas Melville had an even more revealing mania: Customs Officer in the port of Boston and a volunteer fireman, he had a passion for fires: he fought them furiously, more or less deliberately exposing himself to danger – this when he was well over eighty! Certain students of Melville believe that for the Major this was a way of sublimating his robust but declining sensuality which no longer found an outlet.

Regardless, this curious behaviour made him the model for the hero of a highly popular satirical play in New York.

And his descendants definitely inherited some of his extravagance. It was so in the case of Herman's uncle, named Thomas like his father. Thomas, Jr. led a stormy existence. He was living in Paris when the French Revolution broke out. He enjoyed a brief and legendary career as a banker while rubbing friendly shoulders with exiled Republicans such as Joel Barlow and James Monroe. He created quite a scandal in the Melville family when he announced his marriage to a French *dame* who was none other than the adopted niece of Madame Récamier's husband.

This Thomas Melville was an enterprising young man in

Pittsfield at the beginning of the nineteenth century.

every sense of the word. He had a cheerful disposition; he was ambitious; he cultivated the right people, those who led you into the sanctuary of Power. He nonetheless found himself ruined with the end of the Empire. A wife and two children on his hands, he returned to Boston and took up with the Jeffersonians; then he enlisted in the army and was sent to Pittsfield as a commissioner with the rank of Major like his father.

After the War of 1812 Thomas Melville bought a farm there, a modest but authentic domain which he was forced to sell twenty-five years later as his fortunes fast waned.

The man was a real Melville: little gifted for things requiring rigour, Thomas Melville resembled his brother Allan – successes, then – brutally – failure.

To forget his failure, Thomas Melville moved eventually to Illinois where he let the Melvillian extravagance blossom to the fullest. Later, when Herman spent a few weeks at his uncle's house, he described him as an exile from the court of Louis XIV reduced to humble circumstances – far from great and gilded Versailles, from French *savoir-vivre*, from poetry. A little more, Melville added, and he'd have worn a wig!

It is this which must be kept in mind – this heavy Melvillian heritage.

But how could a child have recognized himself in all that? Surrounded by seven brothers and sisters, by servants and close family, how could Herman Melville have understood himself in all that? How would I like him to have seen his childhood? I try to imagine how he saw it by going back into my own past, but nothing stands out. I can't find the magical events by virtue of which one gains an identity. You depend on your father, your mother, all those around you – what they are is what you become.

We were poor at my house. There were fifteen mouths to feed and Father was often out of work, so right from the start a sense of survival was instilled in us. Starting out with that, you'd know how to climb the social ladder and carve out a spot for yourself; once your place was secure, you then drifted pleasantly into old age. Meanwhile Father didn't sleep nights but spent them wide awake biting his nails in the big rocking chair that helped him think. When I rose at night and went to the bathroom at the far end of the hall, I could see the glow of Father's cigarette in the dark. I didn't understand why Father stayed up, though I finally concluded that it was one of his jobs; it was up to him to protect the house during the night. My tranquillity came from Father's misunderstood anguish.

When Father took sick, which happened often since we were always in need of money, I unconsciously made a connection between work and illness: it was quite simple – I didn't want to grow up because then I wouldn't have to work and so would never be sick. That man lying in bed, shaken by spasms, with the white bed pan beside him – that was Father who left each morning to do something I was ignorant of; it lasted all day and sent him home at night worn out, vomiting and racked by convulsions.

How could I have known that Father had to do it? I'd have preferred him to stay at home and have fun with us, invent games so we wouldn't have to grow up too soon. And I would think, 'Maybe it's normal to have ulcers when you're the Father.'

And even as Abel Beauchemin writes, I think, 'If Father had died during one of his attacks, what would have happened? What would the shock have done to me? I don't wish to speak of happiness or sorrow because I don't believe a child knows such terms – simple consciousness, that is, experience, creates the division, splits the universe in two. Before, there is only a single being storing up enough knowledge to gain memory and with it to choose himself. And it's by language that one reaches the threshold, and it's by language that perhaps one can cross over it, within that same language – the sovereign place of secret speech which Herman Broch describes at the end of *The Death of Virgil*:

... the word hovered over the universe, over the nothing, floating beyond the expressible as well as the inexpressible, and he, caught under and amidst the roaring, he floated on with the word, although the more he was enveloped by it, the more he penetrated into the flooding sound and was penetrated by it, the more unattainable, the greater, the graver and more elusive became the word, a floating sea, a floating fire, sea-heavy, sea-light, notwithstanding it was still the word: he could not hold fast to it and he might not hold fast to it; incomprehensible and unutterable for him: it was the word beyond speech.

Broch's description of the Word is about what's left for me of Melville's childhood – a place I can only grasp in space and time by making that space and time my own; but we would then be speaking of something entirely different. So I'm forced to conclude that I'm helpless: Herman Melville's childhood remains up in the air. We won't be out of it before the father's faltering business ends in bankruptcy. That happens in 1830, and takes up almost all of the next chapter. Before getting there I, capricious biographer, put out my hand to receive another cup of coffee which Father offers me in silence.

5

I'm not yet where I believe myself to be, even when I am. For the country I inhabit is devastated and incoherent, shapeless as animal guts – leaving me alone with my furious passion for Melville. So I linger somewhat absurdly at Melville's childhood, at the image I keep of his father, at everything which through him convinces me of his inevitable role in *Moby-Dick*'s failure. With my nose high in the air I watch Father without really seeing him; I allow my mind to wander, content to drift that the shadows of evening might vanish.

When Melville was born, Allan Melville was an exporter. His business was good. It must have been, because in 1821 he moved into a large house on Bleecker Street in Greenwich Village. The house was constantly full of people; and Melville's eyes were already giving him trouble. Odours are so naturally full of memories. There was the pungent smell of Allan Melville's cigars, of Maria's scented dresses:

> I preferred to bury my head in Anna's skirts. And how well I remember the smell of horse droppings carried on the East wind. On Sunday the house came alive because the entire family would spend the afternoon with us. There must have been talk of changes in the nation. I was too young to understand it. Even too young to understand what it meant when Andrew Jackson became President in 1828.

I read this note and stare at the window which has become a hollow large black hole. All I see are layers of fog riven with streams of light. And I think of early America, of what Jacques Ferron used to say to me on the subject before he decided to become a doctor like Chekhov, passionately interested as he was in what lay between history and story. One day he brought me a curious little work entitled *Recherches philosophiques sur les Américains*. A good monk of the eighteenth century, having plundered the libraries of Europe, locked himself in his cell to write the definitive history of the discoveries in America, a sort of anthology of the explorers' stupidity and of the myths they had spawned in order to justify their voyages. I remember only certain details, but the book was a collection of fables. Dom Pernety described the Savages as having holeless bottoms – so they lived off water. Others were one-legged and thus ran two at a time. The Savages were much shorter than Europeans because of the atmosphere – higher than four feet from the ground it became harmful. As for frogs – some weighed close to fifty pounds. As for black people, why Dom Pernety had a theory about them too: each generation was born white but then came down with a jaundice of sorts which, at infancy's end, turned them solidly black.

I don't know why, but I would have liked to speak of all this with Melville and Nathaniel Hawthorne if only to verify my theory that new worlds get discovered no other way. America couldn't escape stupidity. It couldn't have been otherwise because its discovery and foundation were the work of several large families who quickly took over. In Connecticut, for example, ten families ruled between 1662 and 1776. During that period the Walcotts won sixty-nine of the one hundred and forty-four elections held. But the Pitkins did even better – they lost only six. In the Council of Virginia twenty-three families held sixty-three percent of the seats between 1680 and 1776. In New York the Council was monopolized by the financial aristocracy. In Boston ten percent of the population owned sixty percent of the real wealth. It was the same in Virginia: half the inhabitants of that colony were without property or possessions. Even the Western lands were closed to all but the circle of rich, well-established

The force and might of North America portrayed by an eighteenth-century artist.

Eastern speculators. You couldn't just join this magic circle: power always proceeds by exclusion. Until 1763 a royal proclamation forbade colonial settlers to emigrate west of the Appalachians. Because the rich merchants had to get their hands on the land first so that from New York and Boston they could put the whole country under their capitalistic thumb. The Melvilles and the Gansevoorts, if not in the front rank, were well enough placed in this group to enjoy certain advantages. They were glad of their gain, this world of big conservative bourgeois – the blood of business binding them to each other. They were America, the very image of its white future, the crux of the whole matter of *Moby-Dick* on the high Pacific seas.

Thus the importance in American history, in Melville's own life, of Andrew Jackson. Until he was elected President, the American dream had belonged to the East, to those several large families from Washington to New York who handled the affairs of the nation as though they were their own. Look at the White House before Jackson: President John Quincy Adams rose at five every morning; he dressed and, rain or shine, took an eight-mile walk around Washington. Back at the White House he would light his own fire and read three chapters from the Bible annotated by Scott and Henlett; then it was the papers and breakfast. Only once this ritual was over did he receive visitors. He was in bed by eleven every night.

There you have the East before Jackson: the prophets, work, the family. A closed world of settled ideas which Rousseau and the Encyclopedists had whittled away at, obliging the big conservative bourgeois to become liberals. The Melvilles and the Gansevoorts had just climbed aboard the train. At the end of the track waited Andrew Jackson, the first American President not to belong to the East and its trusts. With him cowboys came to the White House. Soon they were playing poker there with guns on the table and girls on their knees. Then the Midwest was invented, forcing the traditional commerce of the East to move its way, getting caught up in Mr. Jackson's herd of wild broncos. Unless they were rich or able to foresee quickly what was happening, the old aristocracy just had to hang on for dear life. The levelheaded Gansevoorts succeeded; the unstable Melvilles went under while producing a witness of their decline – that writer of a Melville who blew all the fuses, including his own.

I must seem to wander but I'm well within the subject of this chapter: we can't understand what Melville wrote if we don't know what took place in America in the 1820s. Without that knowledge Allan Melville's bankruptcy would be inexplicable. And that alone – the bankruptcy – tells me how Melville, in Sartre's words, came to turn himself entirely into an imaginary being, finding his person in the projections of the mind in order to integrate what would have otherwise been unintegrable. Sartre says of Flaubert that he came to grips with himself as a *character* not as a person. Melville did the same. I note what he says of his father:

> I loved him. He was the only one to ever do more than merely inquire about me. When he was on a trip he always had something special to say to me, while for my brothers and sisters he relied on the usual greetings. I was happy, I didn't ask for as much. There were eight of us at home; though I wasn't the eldest, I was my Father's favourite. When you're five years old you don't ask why, you simply take. You ask questions later.

Later – at the time of the father's bankruptcy which was as predictable as the plot of an old French film. In 1829 Allan Melville was still living off what his family had established. Both hands bound to the past, ten mouths to feed, a failing business, a half-mad grandfather who could no longer absorb the biggest debts – there's the situation.

I imagine the days preceding this most important event for Melville. Of course, the children weren't told; but Augusta, Melville's sister, had overheard snatches of conver-

John Quincy Adams,
sixth president of the United States,
1825-1829.

President Andrew Jackson,
symbol of a new America.

sation. And then, Allan Melville had become a different man in no time; unmasked by money troubles, he lost his grip and forgot the image he and the family had of himself. His short temper and dark moods showed him up for what he really was: a troubled man spared the charge of irresponsibility till now solely by the family's good fortune. The intelligent Augusta had no trouble tying the loose ends together, and I reflect that she certainly must have told all to her brother – we might as well get ready for the great changes in store.

I imagine, then, the apple trees in flower, and the horses, harnessed to carriages, trotting along Broadway. Melville is with Augusta. They're looking at what's going on in the street. Colours flashing by, shimmering like butterflies. And these men doffing their hats when they meet a woman – why? Melville asks Augusta; she doesn't know either. So Melville pretends, begins to believe; he has a top hat on his head. He doffs it each time a woman goes by. The women ignore him, of course. Melville tires quickly of the game. With Augusta he goes to sit on the steps of the large colonnaded house. Night come, Augusta says, 'It seems we're all going to stay with Uncle Thomas in Albany.' Melville says, 'I don't understand, Augusta.' Augusta says, 'It's like in those stories Uncle Thomas tells about the Savages. They come at night on ponies and ride round and round the house, faster and faster till their arrows catch on fire. Then they shoot them through the windows and you don't need candles then – it's bright as day. And the Savages enter the house on their ponies and take everything they can; they kill the men and make off with the women and children. That's what happens when you go bankrupt.' Melville says, 'Well then maybe we'd better leave for Albany tonight. Then Father won't be killed, and maybe the Savages won't set fire to the house and we'll be able to come back.'

They're sitting on the steps and Augusta is holding Melville's hand. It's hot and the flowering apple trees are flush with birds. How long are they to remain there, fearing the Savages? Until Allan Melville's arrival. He passes rapidly between them, climbing the steps four at a time. He's without his top hat; his forehead is a mat of wet hair. Melville says, 'He must have run a long ways; and without his cigar.' He wants to go inside but Augusta won't release his hand. Melville says, 'Why don't we go warn Father about the Savages?' Augusta says, 'I haven't finished counting the birds.' Melville shudders, his nose already full of the smells of the horde of wild horses.

Then Maria Melville comes out of the house, a large handkerchief in her hand. She knows that Augusta and Melville are sitting on the steps waiting for the coming of the bankruptcy. Her voice trembles as she calls them. 'Hurry! Hurry! We must leave right away before the Savages arrive!'

Melville and Augusta rush into the house. Behind an armchair stands Allan Melville stiff and straight as a board, his hand resting on the chair's back. The large ring glistens on his finger. He stares straight ahead of him. He says, 'Go away, children. Go away.' They leave him there alone behind his armchair and go up to their rooms. If only the Savages wouldn't come tonight! Tomorrow they would pack their bags, some men would come and put everything in big crates, cart the furniture away – then the whole tribe would climb aboard the large canalboat for Albany. It would be so simple. But since he's found out about the bankruptcy, Melville isn't sure of anything. The bed he is lying in is spinning like a top. He can't sleep. All those scenes rushing through his mind. All those scenes that I, Abel Beauchemin, recreate in order to forget that I'm burning the candle a bit low, Father sitting slumped in sleep beside me.

First, there's the word 'London'. What did Allan Melville say about London? It escapes me now. So much water to cross before the ship docks at Liverpool, before the first harpooned whale he ever saw as he strolled along the deck. When he returned from France he brought with him that glass ship which was kept in a glass case – it was Maria who insisted they place it high on the mantelpiece: all those blue-

Broadway, New York City, 1826.

jacketed sailors, those batteries of cannon Melville never tired of looking at when they left him alone in front of the chimney. He writes:

> I do not know how to account for it, but whenever I looked at it I would feel a desire to be the death of that glass ship, case and all; I wanted to take those small black cannons in my hands, to stuff my pockets with the little blue-jacketed sailors. An insane desire. I shouldn't have told Augusta. She was still a child. She went and told all to Mother. Then Mother removed the ship in its case from the mantelpiece; when I wake up I won't know where it is.

Thus Melville dreams as the night stretches endlessly over them all. Melville doesn't know yet that tomorrow morning hoarfrost will lie atop the lawns of Bleecker Street. How could summer end so brutally? Yesterday hadn't he run with Augusta under the apple trees gathering large bouquets of pink flowers? But how could Melville understand the seasons? One day you woke up and looked out your window and there was snow on the ground. Another day you woke up and looked out your window and there was sunshine everywhere and trees full of large green leaves. No way you could know it wouldn't stay like that forever. As yet you knew nothing of the seasons and the repetitive movement thus etched on the world. Though, in fact, all was stillness when you knew how to see through the seeming movement and beyond that which appeared to be its cause. The succession of days was mere illusion since all it brought were still other days, and days again. Taken together it became hazy and blurred, neutral, so to speak, though in the interstices lay various privileged moments possessed by memory – such a poor instrument with which to learn the truth about oneself! There wasn't much chance of it anyway – you grew old so quickly, like Major Melville who would soon be a hundred. No one dared call him mad for they felt too much pity for him; a Melville walking the streets of Boston in knee-breeches and a tri-cornered hat, such a laughable sight that a

Anonymous. The handsomest ship of the line.

playwright modelled a comic hero on him – wasn't this a definite design, a sign pointing Melville straight to the quiet heart of sorrow?

October.

It was in October 1830 that the Melvilles left Bleecker Street for Albany. Melville's seven sisters and brothers were sent on ahead. Allan Melville kept his beloved son with him. Why? Because Melville couldn't yet take care of himself? Because he was cultivating his passivity and still had difficulty speaking? What did Allan Melville see in his son which he saw in himself as well? What secret consanguinity intuitively understood in troubled times?

> Father and I were alone all that day in the large ravaged house. He remained seated, methodically mopping his brow because of the sweat that was matting his hair. Then the bailiff took the chair out from under him. Father gave him the keys to the large colonnaded house; his hands trembled so much he kept them hidden in his pockets. Night came. I went with

Father to the Cortland Street docks and we waited for the boat that would take us to Albany. We went aboard and Father made me sit on his knees. That way I wasn't able to see his face. That way I could only look in front of me.

Perhaps Melville already understood what was happening, perhaps he knew what they were heading for on the wave-tossed boat that tempestuous night between New York City and Albany. Given all that Augusta had told him about bankruptcy, innocence removed its own blinders. To see this large canalboat plowing through the darkness as they sat shivering in their wet jackets. An initiatory night for Melville as the storm raged round them in booming thunder and bright bolts of lightning that rived the sky. Upon one of these he saw his father's face turned towards the dark wide waters to hide how red, how swollen his eyes were. His father seemed so small and Melville felt like crying, his hands stuck deep within his jacket pockets. When they got to Albany he would no longer be that little boy from Bleecker Street. When they got to Albany Melville would no longer be a little boy: this rough boat trip upriver would put an end to that and bring on monotonous adolescence – bring on all that henceforth would be complicated and uncertain in the Albany fog, the last rung of the father's descent into humiliation. Melville writes:

> How difficult it will be for Father! How I wish he weren't forced to live in Albany! But he's powerless, and I, I count for nothing. I am simply here sitting on his knees aboard this big wave-slapped boat; I am almost asleep, my head resting against Father's shoulder; and I am afraid. I won't eat this apple in my jacket pocket; and I'll speak of none of it to Augusta when we get to Albany; I won't tell her that Father is crying all the time even if there are no tears on his cheeks. There's a worm in the apple I'm carrying in my jacket pocket. And it's windy and raining and thundering, and I would like to forget it all – this big canalboat, Father's knees, those large red eyes fixed on nothing.

William Wall. *The Hudson near Fishkill.* (New York Public Library.)

Leviathan of old.

6

It was James Joyce who said that life is merely a series of interchangeable coincidences, and that that is the stuff of which we're made – that makes us, in Sartre's words, what we were already.

In the days following the Melvilles' move to Albany, the face of the world turned ugly. Gone was childhood in the large colonnaded house in New York City! Gone the tame games played amid plenty! Most pitiful was the fall of the house of Melville! Consider: after installing his family in a banal dwelling a short distance from the Gansevoorts' large house, Allan Melville sank what money he had left in a furrier's shop. Thus began the hand-to-mouth existence the father regarded as the final humiliation. Unable to overcome it, he accumulated debts and frustrations like a final gathering of that ancestral extravagance, culminating in him now, meaning that the old Scottish line of ascendance had been the last of their kind. Twenty years later Melville bears witness to this fact.

As I write Father pours me another cup of coffee. He doesn't quite see what I'm up to in this book. I urged him to read *Moby-Dick* but he didn't get very far because his eyes don't permit him to read.

Once in a while Father peers over my shoulder and reads a few sentences aloud. He obviously doesn't understand. I don't mean what drives me to write, something without which I wouldn't want to exist. He doesn't understand the furious way I'm going about it. He pictures me rather in a small house somewhere with Judith, say, and children and a steady job. Not that he wants me to be like everyone else. On the contrary. He speaks of my talents and how many get used up without compensation each time I write. He says, 'When I'm no longer around, where will you go?' I shrug my shoulders. He says, 'My poor Abel, what will you do with yourself then?'

I set the cup aside and let the felt-tip pen fall upon the page. How Father seems to be wasting away! His tiny arm, I see his tiny arm at the end of the table and consider how weak Father's hold on life is, how far gone he is. Then I reply that what interests me is the image one has of oneself which, despite everything, one clings to with all one's might. It has nothing to do with the outside world. I tell him about Melville's father and the two years he lived in Albany after going bankrupt in New York City; I speak of his desperate efforts to keep his self-image from getting blurred.

I tell Father also that it was no different in his case – substitute Montréal-Nord for Albany and he would be Melville *père*. I say that he too wanted to preserve the image of himself and of his family, an image he thought was his true reflection. I say, 'But in Melville's case it didn't work.' Father answers that it's that way for all of us and that nothing can survive for long unless it's protected. I say, 'But you're all alone like me, like Allan Melville during those two years in Albany, dictated to by the fight for survival, killing yourself because of it.'

Father shrugs his shoulders and lines up a dozen Village cookies to soak in his coffee one at a time. He says, 'That's not the point; the point is the children. You don't maintain that image for yourself alone but for your children, for what's to be brought forth from them.'

I understand then that he wants me to tell him more about Melville – thinking it the best way I have or can have of telling him about myself. Father would like me to tell him how Herman Melville was, how he viewed his father during the two years spent in Albany. If I were to answer him I'd wind up

Anonymous. He who tills his field shall be rewarded.

talking about myself, putting myself in Melville's place, recognizing myself in him and finding again the child I used to be. Perhaps we take such passionate interest in others because reading them alienates us – we discover so many likenesses and set about deliberately developing them in order to enjoy an ultimately treacherous permanence which sinks steadily backward into regression.

    Like Melville, I was a child when Father went bankrupt – out of work and without hope. Things had come to such a pitiful pass that he had to sell the big house at Trois-Pistoles and move to the high country of Saint-Jean-de-Dieu, country which meant nothing to him because it was only Mother's, country he didn't know and would never make his own. Father had never milked a cow, he knew nothing of the seasons or of animals; he was ignorant of what a man sought from the earth in springtime and of its life-giving nature. Mother would laugh at him when he cut his trees six feet from the ground because he didn't know how to pack down snow, making for incredible-looking fields. She saw all he could never become – his profound ineptness for working the land. So she called upon grandfather. Only he knew how to castrate a young pig and shear sheep and plow the land the right way. Only he was a true begetter.

I listen to Father as he tells me all this and wonder in turn what he's up to. He says, 'But it's only important to me. For Mathilde to take my place touched me and left me feeling hurt, too, in my loneliness. That's evident. And sometimes when I got angry I would go at her with everything in me that she dominated. When I calmed down I felt slightly ridiculous because I told myself that the rest of you, like your Melville in Albany, you were alive nonetheless. What could you know of your father's servitude?'

Provoked by his curiosity I set aside the Melville books which earlier I went and got from under my bed. I drop a small sugar cube in my cup of coffee; I take a Village cookie, nibbling it round its ridged edge first as Mother always did, then dipping the rest in my coffee before swallowing it. I need to gain time. Because Father's question doesn't just raise the problem of childhood. And even if it were only that, it would still be a present childhood, as it were, the one I've been living since I returned to Father's house to develop a new rapport between us. It's hard to say what I mean. Suppose I were to look at the problem another way, from the wrong end, even if I seemed once again to be getting off the subject.

All writing reflects passivity, your feminine side. You don't fecundate words: they themselves are both swarming seed and the thing met. Words which violate you and possess you, creating themselves traitorously in your image and likeness – to fool you like the bearded lady in the circus: femininity pushed to the limit.

Father was born and raised in a world of women. All my aunts played music magnificently and painted watercolour landscapes on glass. I could never learn to play music – 'You're not delicate enough,' Father would say. He could play, however. It was the only thing, in fact, that he was better at than Mother: come from a family of village musicians, like me she never learned to play. Yet she loved music as much as I. When she was still alive and I was having all those problems with Judith, I would come once in a while to the house: neither of us needed to speak because Father played for us. Like softness enveloping us, Father's unique tenderness giving us something we would never possess on our own: femininity. I felt big and clumsy when I left Father's house, carrying with me that tranquil image of him in his easy chair with his long, fine hands holding the harmonica, his undershirt hanging off his shoulder. That white, smooth Eskimo skin.

Impertinent or not, to really understand Father's question I have to say that I've always thought of him as my mother – and of Mother as my father. Physically, I resemble Mother. Like her, I'm stout, large-boned, strong in the leg, large in the seat, and sway-backed. At fourteen I was taller and better built than Father. He took after his sisters, who would say when they saw each other at New Year's, 'How cute Charles is!' He was adolescence hanging on somehow.

As far back into my childhood as I can go, I can't remember Mother being soft with me. It was Father who rocked and cradled me; it was with him that I studied my lessons. Mother was on the side of the school: she wanted me to write with my right hand. I was more afraid of her than I was of the schoolmistress – she would sit across the table from me and stare at me with eyes that seemed to say, 'Try. Just to see.' Mother also who because I was still wetting the bed at five years and more would chase me into the kitchen with a thick switch in her hand, yelling like a madwoman. Father would calm us both down, saying, 'It's not his fault. Bouscotte's not responsible for any of it. Leave him alone.'

That's how it was. Even sickness – which has a feminine social function – it was Father who got sick. He was the one who had the stomach aches and spent nights vomiting into the bedpan, his body raised to spew out the food it had taken in. Of course, Mother had trouble for a long time with one of her legs. But it was a superficial, an open wound. It had nothing to do with the fact that she was a woman. Perhaps everything I'm saying stems from the fact that as a child I believed it was the father who made the children. Every time it occurred, Mother was playing a peculiar game with us. I was certain she had strapped a pillow to her belly to trick us just as grandmother used to do.

Which is to say that after the first great disturbance which saw us leave Trois-Pistoles for the heights of Saint-Jean-de-Dieu, this ambiguity was confirmed: Mother gave the orders: it was she who knew when the hay must be mowed; she who knew when the fences must be mended; she who knew in which direction to plow; she who knew how to slaughter hogs; she who knew what price to ask for the animals. Father's authority was limited to the horse, a handsome stubborn beast he must have chosen precisely because it was a rebel and hardly manageable, he being the only person it would listen to. Mother always stood in horror of horses.

But I have to admit that my childhood wasn't in the least disturbed by Mother's dominance; it only drove me closer to

Father. Perhaps Father was as young as we and that was why he played so many games with his children, unheeding of Mother who said he was wasting time. Father's fortunate childishness!

When I try to explain that to him he laughs. His small shoulders pump up and down. He thinks I'm making it up. He hasn't yet understood that since I've come back to the house I've been playing the idealized role of Mother. I do the dishes and keep house; I do Father's laundry, do the shopping and make the beds. In return Father provides for me. I didn't want it to come to that but Father insisted so much I finally gave in. He said, 'That's all I'm good for now, to try to make things possible. All the better if because of me you can write that book about your friend Melville.'

My friend Melville! Father speaks of Melville as though we were the same age. He can't imagine that Melville is an aged man, far older than he will ever be. When I tell him that I find this identification between writing and youth rather curious, he says, 'But it's simple. When you're really old you can't do anything. You watch others, happy if you can be of service.'

Father's gotten in my way. I'm afraid I'm a bit off the track. If I listened to myself I'd drop Melville and write about Father, something I promised him I wouldn't do till after his death. He says, 'Excuse me, I didn't mean to disturb you.'

For a while he'll pretend to retire for the night, slipping on his pyjamas and stretching out on his bed. How could he sleep knowing I'm here at the apple-tree wood table tying it all together? Later he'll come back and sit beside me with the large family album on his lap – Father's way of preparing the long novel we're no doubt going to write together after *Monsieur Melville*. Father raises his eyes. He sees me looking at him. He says, 'Stop fooling around, Abel. If you want to finish that chapter before morning you'd better roll up your sleeves.'

Anonymous. *Brother and Sister*. About 1845.

7

I had got up to Allan Melville's death, to the long months of bitterness preceding it. Melville himself dwells upon those events, especially in *Redburn*. I'll show this later. At the moment I merely note a couple of passages I came across in my reading. They show clearly where the bankruptcy had left the family. Melville says:

> It was sadness itself. Father went to work in his fur store while I continued in school. I was a fair student but woefully ill-at-ease with my studies. Whenever the school organized festivities I would recite Byron. And then there was Cousin Guert and Uncle John De Wolf who spoke endlessly of their adventures at sea – as if that could have made us forget Father's fall. The whole time, we were living in that new house in Albany as though it and all the rest were ours on loan. The storm had to break at some point.

It broke in January 1832. One evening Allan Melville came home terribly worked up: he went straight to bed never to leave it again, charging that ultimate prostration with the weight of his full refusal. His speech grew extravagant and wild, making death all the more alarming. I can easily picture Maria Melville trying to hide the truth from her children, keeping them away from their mad father who had become the captive of the whispering shadows and of the delirium of his end. Melville says:

> I was thirteen when Father died. I was never to live through anything so painful until Malcolm's death. Father now dead,

how could I exist, *be*? Until age twenty-five I regarded myself as an irresponsible creature, as one incapable of answering for himself. Nothing seemed to move; reality itself was deficient and I was incapable of action. As opposed to my brother Gansevoort who quit school upon Father's death to go into business – the fur business. He had a card printed – 'G. Melville, Dealer in Furs, and Manufacturer of all Descriptions of Fur, Cloth, Morocco & Fancy Corps.' And then the inevitable happened: Gansevoort went bankrupt, he also – before he was twenty! He left Albany then to start up again in Lansingburgh, and my sisters took in sewing so we could live.

To understand the extent to which his father's death was the capital event which put an end to Melville's childhood, one must read *Pierre,* written immediately after the failure of *Moby-Dick.* It was no accident that he chose to speak of his family, placing the unsettling image of the father at the very centre of his book. Not three decades distant, the symbolism is transparent: after the father's failure the son's must follow. The same thing occurs when Malcolm puts a bullet in his brain – Melville breaks his long silence as a novelist to write *Billy Budd.*

Melville maintains this identification with his father right to the end; it becomes particularly important in the years following *Moby-Dick.* With the result that in 'Bartleby, the Scrivener' – that strange, singular tale – he is both his father and himself, a veritable Janus of dispossession and of passive and absolute refusal. No one has looked closely enough at that work, a work that shows Melville at the heart of his failure, at his most desperately *neutral.* 'Bartleby, the Scrivener' supports Sartre: in that work, like Flaubert in *Madame Bovary,* Melville reveals his deepest nature – this is a man who, as I have said, approached himself as a *character* and never as a *person.*

I see only this difference between them: Melville kept the

R. Earl. *Family Portrait.* 1804.

separation secret while Flaubert made it the central affair of his life. Sartre writes:

> On the other hand, what Flaubert feels *for himself*, the lived, disqualified as it is, seems to him the least-part-of-being, unessential and, in a way, lacking reality since this felt thing is crude, inconsistent stuff whose only function, once elaborated, is to serve his public character.

In other words, Flaubert devotes himself to the representation of his being, especially after the epileptic fit at Pont-L'Évêque which led him to say 'that his very being had been spirited away and that he was no one any more'. As a child, Flaubert regarded himself as the idiot of the family who would remain unimportant because reality belonged to others. Flaubert too, then, absolutely refused *to be*. His childhood over, not only is he convinced that he cannot, but he persuades himself that he must not *be*; it is as though his life were already behind him, spent in the death-dealing fullness of the family. There you have why he begins to write at ten years of age. There you have why between ten and fifteen years of age he writes stories in which he shows how he has chosen once and for all to see himself. Sartre says:

> But things are such with him that he can understand himself only by inventing himself. Thus, from this period on literature becomes his salvation since for him it is pure self-invention; setting down his fantasms, he manages to overcome, if only confusedly, his own chaotic heart, to soar in unreality high above his real situation.

Become literally an imagination, Flaubert conceived the dream of *Madame Bovary*, that total, definitive book.

I dwell upon all this because of the coincidences. Sartre finds his double in Flaubert; and if in this book I do as much with Melville, it's because I haven't lost my passion for serial writing. For literature to be created because of one's inability to speak is of the utmost importance. Reality is made manageable through writing, through the reciprocity, the various rapports that constitute writing. It's this very reciprocity, these various rapports, that get profoundly changed: at one and the same time, it's yourself and something other than yourself-always-yourself that make up the first and last terms of written discourse: Sartre calls it 'totalized unrealization'.

On this level Melville resembles Flaubert; *Moby-Dick* is *Madame Bovary*. Obviously each man took a different road: Flaubert's love for his father went unrequited while Melville's idolized father worshipped him, too. Flaubert looked upon his father as an obstacle to his ever becoming more than he was – a superfluous creature whom the family could have, should have done without; Melville shouldered the very stuff of becoming, took on the transparency of his father's image. The begetter dead, in Melville dies all memory. After the father's death it was all over, Melville's well of feeling dried up: the next sixty years change nothing of that, they leave untouched the being who at thirteen was sealed off behind refusal by Allan Melville's death.

Though at first glance Flaubert's and Melville's ways of proceeding may seem different, they are in fact identical even though one is the reverse of the other. Flaubert invents himself in childhood while Melville does so only once he is an adult. The result is strangely the same and turns into those two phenomenal acts, *Madame Bovary* and *Moby-Dick*. Thus Flaubert and Melville both are like the serpent who swallows his tail: the completed work, that is, the thing that finally made them 'responsible' beings, must at the same time devour them from within, destroying all possibility of continuing. Flaubert died while at work upon *Bouvard et Pécuchet*, a work which raised the problem of knowledge seeking to know itself. And Melville wrote 'Bartleby, the Scrivener' whose meaning, despite the difference in genre (perhaps because of this difference), is as luminously evident as that of *Bouvard et Pécuchet* – much less veiled, in fact, since to the question of knowledge Melville adds the problem of ferocious solitude.

8

Thus I meander through my book on Melville, presenting slowly and singly the pieces I've selected, being in no hurry to get to the end; it's as though I didn't dare proceed directly and were using biography as a means of retreating to the front; trying to remain calm while possessed by a feverish urge to break loose and speak solely of *Moby-Dick*, of beauty so terrible that once in its grasp I'd risk losing myself in whatever I might say, risk seeing my words made meaningless, small, invisible by what is said there.

And all the while I still seek the *how* of Melville, lingering over his childhood in order to arrive at it quietly, creep up on it. But I can no longer be an ordinary reader satisfying his passion in perfectly linear fashion. Certainly not at three o'clock in the morning with Father sound asleep beside me, a slender thread of saliva running through the white stubble on his chin. I'd be better to hit the sack and let my begetter sleep the normal way. Why is he so concerned about what I'm writing, and why has he transformed himself into a discreet and devoted angel keeping silent watch over me? Does he really believe that simply because he's there the book will come more easily?

I place my hand on his arm. He opens his eyes and looks at me as though he'd never seen me before. I say, 'Father, you should go to bed now and get some rest. It's enough for me to stay up.' He says, 'You think so! Two's not so many for an all-nighter. Keep at it, don't bother about me. I was dreaming of the book we're going to write if you don't spend too much time on this one. How far have you got? You think you'll be finished in two or three days?'

I laugh, and Father laughs with me, tilting his chair back as he sits up straight and folds his arms across his chest. When he stops laughing he'll go fix me another cup of coffee. I've gone back to Melville, imagining him in Albany after his father's death; Albany, that overgrown village, the creation of the Gansevoorts who alone stand between the Melvilles and the poorhouse. While waiting for the children, growing up at last, to be able to look after their mother, her reward for being so brave, so courageous.

But it's just as it was with Melville's photograph when I began this book. I start up once more with a fictional fabrication which obliges me to present Melville's adolescence *via* Augusta. Why have I chosen Augusta, and no one else, as Melville's privileged interlocutor? Because she was his sister, of course. And the nearest to him in age. Also, as I'll show later on, because Melville loved Augusta more than any other woman; she became both his confidante and his copyist. In return, Augusta never married so that she might remain with him – until *Pierre or the Ambiguities*, at least. For when Melville left for New York after yet another still-born book, Augusta didn't follow him but moved in with a female relative. Which saw Melville refuse to open his door to her later when he had become Inspector of Customs – he was down with a fever on that occasion; and had already turned into that aged, difficult man who was always in a state of crisis because he was so profoundly alone, his mother, his wife Lizzie and his children serving merely to remind him that he'd made a mess of his life and of the lives of those around him.

There is how I choose to justify my fictional use of Augusta. But perhaps she's only a projection of myself, a simple ruse allowing me to feel closer to Melville and to have a place in his life now that Allan is dead.

But here's Augusta saying, 'Don't worry, Herman, Uncle Peter will find you something. He's doing all he can

The Berkshires.

Sailors boarding a ship in the eighteenth century.

for us. Meanwhile, couldn't we read another chapter of the adventures of Captain Kidd?' Melville answers, 'I'll go get the book, Augusta. Then we'll go sit under the big oak in Longmeadow and take turns reading paragraphs.'

Reading Captain Kidd was much better than doing the homework assigned by Father Mapple of the Albany Academy since that called up desolation and Allan Melville's death.

The book on his knees, Melville thinks, 'Those days preceding Father's death, when everything seemed to be standing still, even the odours which smelled just like the mouldy bread in Uncle Peter's big house. I didn't think Father could go away like that with a wasted look and eyes unwilling to close and Mother crying all the time. Augusta!'

Those animals in Longmeadow, huge clever beasts you can go up to, Augusta rubbing them between their horns. Melville reflects that it's all going to be over soon. Augusta and he are sitting under the oak. But they don't dare open the book right away; it's as though they were waiting: Captain Kidd isn't everything in Melville's life, that is, he doesn't provide its missing dimensions. Then Augusta says, 'Later, what will you do, Herman?' He says, 'I learn so slowly it's going to take a long, long time.' Augusta says, 'Maybe I'll get married. I'll wear long dresses and have somebody like Uncle Peter.' Melville says, 'You're sure to be lucky, Augusta. But if there isn't anybody like Uncle Peter?' Augusta says, 'Then I won't do anything, I'll stay just as I am.' Melville says, 'That's wise, Augusta. Myself, I think I'm going to be bored always.' Augusta says, 'You're funny.' Melville says, 'I don't think I have any talent.' Augusta says, 'Be fair to yourself, Herman. When we go to see you recite at the Albany Academy, it's beautiful. And what you write is fine, too.' Melville says, 'But I can't take the credit. They're Byron's words. He travelled all over the world, Augusta.' She says, 'Uncle John De Wolf has too. He crossed the whole Russian Empire in a sled. He's been on every sea and ocean. But he'll never write anything as fine as you, and you haven't gone anywhere. Take Cousin Guert. When he was twelve years old he was already in the Navy. But he can't tell stories.' Melville says, 'Only Father knew how to tell stories.' Augusta says, 'And Byron.' Melville says, 'I just repeat what others have said. I'm a great big parrot, that's all.' Augusta says, 'A parrot!' Melville says, 'Is it so funny?' Augusta says, 'I heard "parrot" and what I saw was a boat. That's reason enough to laugh, isn't it?'

Then Melville begins to laugh with Augusta, his small blue eyes turned towards the cows making their way to Long's stable. Melville says, 'I don't like this country, Augusta. Since Father's death Mother's rarely in a good mood. She's always wearing a frown except when Uncle Peter comes to see us. Then she gets out the pretty white tablecloth and all the smells from before are there again. I wonder sometimes where Father is now. I wonder when he's coming back. I know he won't ever come back but still I wonder when he's coming back.' Augusta says, 'You have to forget, Herman.' Melville says, 'I can't.' Augusta says, 'But you have to, Herman. If not, it's an offense.' Melville says, 'What are you trying to get across to me?' Augusta says, 'Father wouldn't want us to do otherwise.'

Melville closes his eyes, Captain Kidd's book still on his knees. He doesn't understand what Augusta is saying any more than he understands the words of his other brothers and sisters. Finally, perhaps, one understands nothing. Maybe there isn't any meaning anywhere. The thought passes through Melville's mind. He says, 'Don't leave right away, Augusta. The cows are about to come back. We'll watch them chew the grass.' Augusta says, 'Mother doesn't like us to be late for dinner.' She stands up, shaking the twigs off her dress, and leaves Melville there under the oak, his nostrils wide to the wind.

Afterwards, the dream. Afterwards, Melville's softly flowing thoughts brought on by the smells. 'I'd like things to

stay this way, suspended in twilight, because it's the best time to be under an oak. If I go to sleep maybe I'll wake up completely different, very old and with no memory of what occurred while I was asleep; maybe I'll have white hair down to my knees. When Father died he was holding Mother's hand; he said, "It all goes by so fast it's absurd, so very absurd."'

As the cows graze in Longmeadow Melville nods off, waiting for Uncle Peter who is supposed to take him to New York City where, it seems, he's found Herman a job at the State Bank. Without Augusta. It's going to be difficult and Melville isn't interested. His mother says it's because he doesn't know what he wants to do. For that matter, why not sell hats in Uncle Peter's store? But it's true that Augusta said it would happen. He hears her say, 'Come, Herman. Come.' Captain Kidd's book slides to the ground. Melville is sound asleep.

Before he wakes up we'll be in New York City, and Melville will be bored stiff at the State Bank – so much so that they worry about him, whispering it in order not to alarm him, and charging Uncle Peter with arranging things. On Wall Street the night Uncle Peter left the State Bank with Melville, supposedly to find him new lodgings but in fact to get to the bottom of things, Uncle Peter said, 'You don't like your job at the bank. You're not good at it, you don't apply yourself. You've a future there, however. But I can understand that it's not for you. So what do we do now, Herman?' Melville doesn't answer. The evidence says everything. In any case, he's never felt comfortable with Uncle Peter. All these annoying things he agrees to do to help his mother Maria! He's bent beneath his tiredness. But like the Gansevoorts, he doesn't speak of it. That solid aristocratic ideal, that way of being above one's cares and concerns – and that way Uncle Peter has of looking and taking in all of Albany, New York City, Boston, America. What did Uncle Peter say the other day to John De Wolf? He was speaking of Andrew Jackson, comparing him to John Quincy Adams. He said, 'If all America lived as Adams lived, there wouldn't be this decadence that's threatening to finish off the spirit of the Founding Fathers.' Uncle Peter had spoken at length in his full, calm voice as John De Wolf nodded his sympathy. Sympathy, but no more. He knew from having travelled so widely that you couldn't stem the tide. Instead, they all seemed to be involuntarily caught up in a mad, headlong rush to the ocean where they would disappear in anonymity. Uncle Peter says, 'So what shall we do, Herman?' Melville says, 'I don't know, Uncle Peter.' Uncle Peter says, 'You can't remain in the bank, that's certain. So we have to find you something else, work that will please you.' Melville tries to tell him that that kind of work doesn't exist but the words stick in his throat. Uncle Peter following, he climbs the stairs to his room; it's a banal, lifeless place: this bed, this tiny table, this large brown suitcase belonging to Cousin Guert – nothing of Melville in any of it. Uncle Peter sits down on the bed. The springs squeak. What is he imagining for Melville that he doesn't know how to say? This impression that with

The *Mayflower* pilgrims.

Melville something is always being held back – this disconcerting passivity which eludes apprehension, words seeming not to carry that far; or, rather, flying past and landing against the wall.

Uncle Peter says, 'What's the matter, Herman?' But he doesn't wait for an answer, he doesn't expect any from Melville, not now, not ever. So he picks up Cousin Guert's large brown suitcase and carries it downstairs, Melville following. The new room won't be any better than the old. And even if it were more comfortable, in fact, Melville wouldn't notice. He's not concerned with such things. The fact is he's bored, he's convinced that for the rest of his life he will know this irresolution, this feeble indifference characterizing his every action save the frantic, tumultuous act of writing out of which *Moby-Dick* is to grow, only to come to grief upon the world's neglect.

Uncle Peter says, 'You're seventeen now, Herman. Most boys your age have established themselves. You must find a way.' Melville shrugs his shoulders; as they head for Uncle Peter's hat shop, he stares in the store windows along Market Street. Selling hats is all New York City has to offer a seventeen-year-old Melville, and even then it's due to the Gansevoorts. Without them what a desert the place would be. It already is one for Melville but he doesn't know it yet, occupied as he is in perfecting the process of alienation he's begun, killing off dreams one by one. Soon he won't even know who Byron is, he won't remember the verses that inflamed him at the Albany Academy, that set him on the high adventurous seas at the helm of a brazen explorer's vessel. In New York City you sell hats and remain as bored as before. Augusta's no longer there to go sit with beneath the large oak in Longmeadow and read the adventures of Captain Kidd.

Thus Melville is already writing the first part of *Redburn* in his head. Upon entering Uncle Peter's shop he closes his eyes so as not to see anything, and suddenly he's back in his room idly awaiting Mrs. Gaddis' call to supper. Sundays are longest: when you're broke and seventeen and friendless, Sundays are rough. When I was Melville's age I'd put on my jeans, slip my belt through the holstered knife I'd swiped from my brother, don my leather jacket and go wait for the bus at the stop next to the house. We crossed the town of Rivière-des-Prairies, then Montréal-Nord, then Saint-Michel, then Rosemont. Getting off at the rue Berri terminal, I would hang around for awhile outside Baillargeon Transport or in front of the snack bar next door. When I had a little money I would buy myself a hot dog and wolf it down before boarding another bus which was headed for the port. The tramways were still running in those days but I never took one because of those lines flashing fire, sparks shooting in every direction. I would get off at the Ruelle de la Friponne.* I don't know why, nor what it was about the name that fascinated me so much that I would wind up there even when I meant to go elsewhere. My God, how many times I made that trip! Every Sunday, in fact, just to get as far away from the house as I could and forget my boredom.

Can Melville have spent his Sundays any differently? From what I know I think not, my reading of *Redburn* tells me no. His Ruelle de la Friponne was the fort built by Governor Tomkins on a high cliff in the Narrows. Melville went there often. I had no real reason to go to the Ruelle de la Friponne, but Melville had good ones for his pilgrimages to the fort: before his father's death, they had gone there with Uncle De Wolf – Herman was impressed by the savage countryside, by the thick walls, by all that endures even in ruin. In *Redburn* Melville writes:

> It was noon-day when I was there, in the month of June, and there was little wind to stir the trees, and everything looked as if it was waiting for something, and the sky overhead was blue as my mother's eye, and I was so glad and happy then.

* Rogue's or (in Beaulieu's sense) Delinquent's Alley [Tr.]

> But I must not think of those delightful days, before my father became a bankrupt, and died, and we removed from the city; for when I think of those days, something rises up in my throat and almost strangles me.

Thus the memory Melville kept of the few months he lived in New York City between the State Bank and Uncle Peter's hat shop. *Everything looked as if it was waiting for something* – it's this sentence that speaks to me, by it that Melville reveals himself: in New York City he was nothing, turned towards the past and childhood and waiting for something to happen which would shake up his life. Poor Melville! It took him weeks and weeks to understand that he was living in a state of pure indifference and solitude, not knowing which way to turn and with no way out.

It could have gone on for an entire lifetime, Melville mutely living the drama of Bartleby the scrivener.

Something occurred, however, in the spring of 1836. There's no word of it in the biographies of Melville but I'm sure something happened in the spring of 1836, something important enough for Melville to leave his job as hat salesman and return to Albany. Couldn't it have been a quarrel with Uncle Peter who was fed up with his nonchalance and his lack of interest in his work? What truths was Uncle Peter able to show him about himself? It must not have been very gay for Melville – I even suspect it was what, back in Albany, caused him to seek refuge at Uncle Thomas' house where he spent the summer helping in the fields. Broadwall was still rich: an English colonial house with a cellar full of wine, firewood and potatoes, attics full of fruit and old trunks, rooms full of books and paintings. Presiding over it all like an old baron was the uncle, Thomas Melville, proprietor of an American domain and master of a French wife with whom he took long walks and engaged in conversation, a lord of the manor fluent in the French tongue. In some ways, Melville's universe before the father's fall was an eccentric world, an

Cannibals preparing for a feast.

extravagant society whose peculiar nature was shown fully only later.

At Broadwall Melville got to know his cousin Thomas who, at thirty, had travelled around the globe as an officer in the American Navy; he took sick at some point and was forced into early retirement. The Melvilles lacked stamina. But what stories Thomas could tell, drawing on his adventures and his encyclopedic culture to excite your imagination and keep you rapt. Ah, those cannibals on Typee that Thomas really saw, he says! Ah, Honolulu and Tahiti, virgin islands, the threshold to paradise! A whole bevy of facts and delicious anecdotes that Melville must have listened to religiously with guilty discretion, he the hard times cousin with no story to tell, a hired hand good for feeding the animals and for harvest jobs. Because Melville was lucid enough to see that he was a stranger nonetheless for these people, even if he shared their roof. He didn't have his parents' polish, he knew nothing about anything. He didn't belong in these people's world, though he carried it inside him. So, inevitably, he fled into the past, into the enchanted past of his father. Into that vicious circle from which, a final time, he tried to escape by leaving his uncle's house for a teaching post in a country school. Nothing of that winter was to survive except his decision to finally take to the high seas once the snow had melted – to throw himself into the sea, as he has written, meaning thereby that his undertaking couldn't compare with what his illustrious cousins had done.

In the spring of 1839 when Melville boarded ship for Liverpool, he was merely filling an inner need: emptiness was sapping his life and perhaps the sea could finally give some meaning to it. When you're poor you've got no choice. Melville was to have other occasions to learn this.

9

Father says, 'You're being unreasonable, Abel. You ought to go lie down for a while. Twenty hours straight you've been sitting there writing. What's the hurry?'

What can I say? That I want to finish as quickly as possible with Melville's adolescence and get to the quiet heart of his unhappiness as he reaches his thirties and there's no more compensation, neither at sea nor in writing novels? But I'm knocked out, swallowed, worn out by what I've written so far. I'm unable to take on the things about Melville's life that don't really interest me. If only there weren't these mechanical failures – fingers that grow stiff, a hand that refuses to move, and the body along with it; it slows me down and sets limits to my undertaking that I can't get around; thus, much of my pleasure is lost and in its place comes this futile fury, this revolt by what in me refuses to sleep! This book has to be written in a single sitting, I can't rest before it's finished. That way I can reach another, non-linear stage at last, break open my sentences, open them wide like a female womb and fecundate the book, or rather what the book shall have become, namely, a prodigious, timeless force. Writing's so very slow! It's so difficult to give it your all!

Sitting at this apple-tree wood table, I feel like a limp dishrag, no strength left in me now. After each sentence I feel such tiredness; I'm thoroughly drained. Judith understood no more than Father what goes on inside me when I enter this perilous state in which identity vanishes and one becomes another. For two years I was Victor Hugo, his very image – better, I was a golem aglow with energy, I was both Hugo and myself, I soared in frantic flight from which I landed lost and confused. Afterwards I felt as though I were hoary with age, nearing death. To keep from succumbing, going under, I wrote the book about my grandfathers; it was my only way to get hold of myself. Next came my mad passion for Kerouac; I was drawn to him because anguish filled his writing, because his origins had left him in such a narrow pass, because it was impossible for him *to be* except through misunderstanding. I worked on the book seventeen hours a day, rising in the morning to fall to the task like a man possessed; my fever almost did me in before the work was completed – that brutal arrival of the ambulance which took me to Sacré-Coeur Hospital, into Don Quixote's rubbery world; it appeared in the night like a sneer so that in chasing after it I might forget Kerouac and the madness he'd introduced into my life. How right Judith was to leave me then! Strictly speaking, I was merely one long blind word. I'd have been the death of her had she stayed; unawares, I'd have gobbled up her whole life because of the writing always going on inside me, because of what I'm borne by – I have to put it in writing though I know failure awaits me, the impossibility of being, the very thing that stokes my passion for Melville, bringing me back to Father's house unburdened of my characters to become this naked image, this medium eating up time and space to get at the creator of *Moby-Dick* – to lose myself, in other words, and him with me.

Father insists that I go to bed. He's placed his two hands on my shoulders as though about to drag me away from the table and put me to bed himself. I stay on, however, though I haven't written anything for quite a while. Father says, 'You're just not being reasonable, Abel. Save something for tomorrow. Your friend Melville doesn't expect so much. You should get some sleep now.'

My hand won't let go of the felt-tip pen, my eyes continue to stare at the unspoiled page, my mind is blank. Nothing can bring me out of it, not even Father. My body's as thin

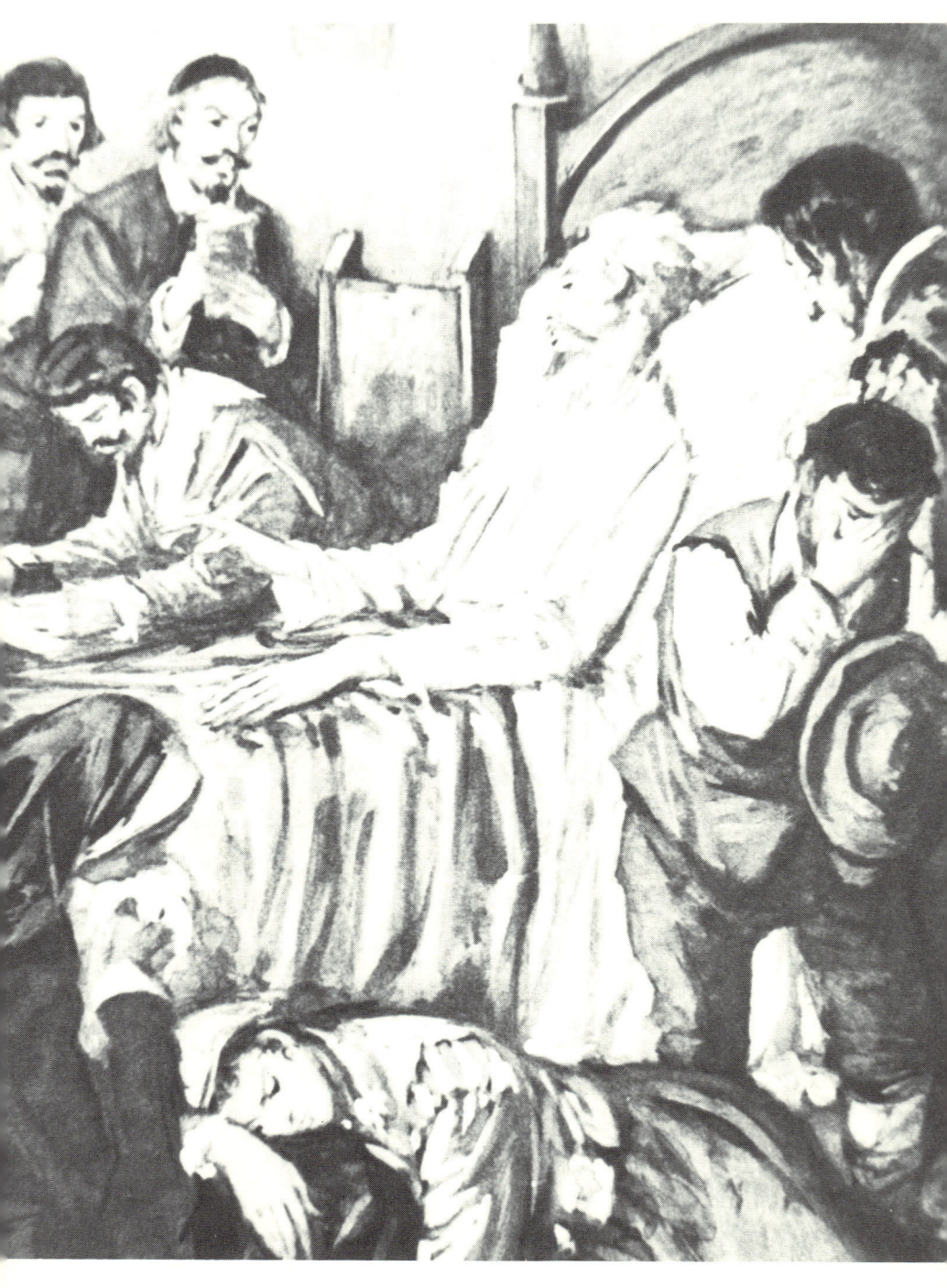

as a razor's edge, I'm just conscious enough still to wonder what will happen when shortly I arrive at Melville's ancient Arrowhead, a place hollowed out by the incisive tones of pain and fear. But I don't want to think about that yet, so I say, 'Give me some more coffee, a large cup to signal the end. Then I'll take a break.'

Before I finish drinking it they knock on the door, two tiny raps so discreet that Father and I don't hear them. We're sitting side by side in silence over our coffees, perhaps a bit sad at finding nothing to say which would soothe us and give us back our complicity. How can I explain to Father, make him see clearly, when I myself don't fully understand?

Two more knocks on the door. Father goes to answer. I hardly notice; my head is heavy with sleep. Father says, 'Abel! Abel! You'll never guess who's here!' I stand up, unsteady on my feet. The first thing I see is a crutch at the far end of the hallway. Then a leg swings into view bound in splints. I shout, 'France! Is it you? France! France! You promised me. ...' Then things begin to swim before my eyes,

my body goes completely limp, I fall down in a heap.

I come to in an easy chair; on my forehead is a cold compress. France stands looking at me. Job J too. And Una, who is sitting on the floor between her father's legs. Samm has her back turned to me (for though I've never laid eyes on her I know her by the mass of black hair framing her body and by her tight-fitting nurse's uniform which renders her body transparent). I say, 'I didn't expect you so soon. I even thought you wouldn't ever come back.' Job J says, 'Samm wanted to go to Mattavinie for the weekend. Since we had to come into town we thought we'd stop by and say hello.' I search for Father, looking to the left and to the right to keep from seeing Samm right away. She's staring at me now, the narrow slits of her eyes seeking mine. What is there in Samm's curiosity that makes me feel I've been impaled? She says, 'I'm pleased to make your acquaintance. France told me you were the first person ever to buy one of her paintings. And Job J says you're writing a book on Melville. Do you believe in coincidences? We all read *Moby-Dick* this summer. France lent it to me while she was in the hospital. I'm in love with Queequeg. He should have been saved instead of Ishmael, don't you think?' I say, 'Where's Father?' France says, 'I think he went to get something to drink.' Job J says, 'How's your book coming? Your father told us you were working too much. He said it was crazy.' I laugh, my tiredness suddenly lifted. Maybe it's the waves Samm's sending my way that have relaxed me – they're coming so naturally, free as birds and full of warmth. I say, 'I'm not working too much. It's just that it's a difficult book. It lay dormant too long inside me and I'm having trouble keeping it awake. I mean, what I awaken isn't always what I want to see come out. So many detours!'

Father appears in the hallway carrying a tray of brimming cups of wine. We haven't drunk anything else since I began this book on Melville. When I was writing the Kerouac book I was on Geneva gin. How absurd it all is! My eyes are hurting. I'm going to wind up like Father with lenses thick as a magnifying glass. Una offers me a cup of wine. She must be all of five now. A tiny girl with eyes like dark round marbles that swallow up her face. She's climbed onto my knees, and it seems so strange to me: if Una were blonde she might be Judith's and Julien's daughter back from Florida, a little chunk of sunshine.

Job J says, 'If we're disturbing you, just say so.' I say, 'You're not disturbing me. I'm just dog tired, that's all. I haven't stopped since yesterday and it's hard for me even to think. What's happened since the other night?' France says, 'They took my cast off and I'm learning to walk again. Job J finally finished his documentary for American TV; he's been looking after Una since then. She's got a little roan pony and a whole bunch of chicks that she watches over like a mother hen. Don't worry, there's never a dull moment.' Job J says, 'The old barn in Mattavinie needs a lot of mending and I want to build a windmill.' I say, 'You're lucky to be in the country, even if I can't see myself there.' Father says, 'You didn't seem to mind too much being there on the heights of Saint-Jean-de-Dieu. You didn't even want to come with us when we moved.' I say, 'It wasn't the same thing. I didn't know anything about the world then. I wasn't familiar with the rest. I didn't even know you could run away like that.' Una says, 'Can I have a sip, Abel?' I say, 'Of course, Una. Of course.' She takes a sip, makes a face and hands me my cup. Una! How light she is! The tiny sharp bones of her buttocks stick into my thighs. I say, 'What are you going to be when you get big?' She says, 'Yesterday I was big. Now I'm little. Tomorrow – I don't know. Why are you asking me that?' I say, 'No reason.' She says, 'Then why are you asking?' She pulls my beard, her face pinched as she sits perched on my knees. If it hadn't been for that blood in the bathtub in Gespeg* perhaps Blanche would have given me a little girl like Una. I say, 'And you, Samm, what's happening with you?' She says, 'I'm still working at the hospital but I don't

* Gaspé [Tr.]

know for how long. As Melville says, everybody knows that from eating calves' brains certain epicures wind up without much brains themselves, they confuse a calf's head with their own. That's about the way I view the hospital. But let's speak a little bit about Melville and *Moby-Dick,* all right?' I say, 'For the moment, I can't, I'm not there yet. I've hardly finished Melville's adolescence. Besides, I don't really feel up to it. What I'd say wouldn't have a great deal to do with the mighty whale. Father, a little more wine, please.' He says, 'I should have brought the jug.' Job J says, 'I'll go get it for you.'

He disappears down the hallway. Job J seems to have changed quite a bit since that famous meeting here in Father's house. I didn't realize he was so tall, with those large shoulders and strong thighs that would have served him better if I'd made a wrestler of him rather than first – and sole – citizen of Mattavinie. It all slips through my fingers like sand. Only a week ago I put my characters out to pasture and already they're far away from me in a world which obeys neither time nor space. Soon they'll be beyond my control and God knows what they'll be capable of then in their displaced, thus illogical universe. I look at Samm, who's still almost nonexistent except for the beauty of her body, her odours, that mixture of earth and grass – and I understand why they've come: it's to offer up Samm in sacrifice: I'm feeding off her, her body gives me energy of a much better kind than sleep could provide. The more I stare at Samm the less tired I feel. She's slowly becoming diaphanous. If I do nothing, remain passively soaking up her energy with my eyes, she'll never again leave this house, she'll be unable to move from here, she'll stay like imprisoned matter on the couch where she's sitting cross-legged, wide-eyed. I say, 'Samm, you've got to get out of that hospital. The sooner the better. Nobody should let herself become institutionalized.' I don't know why I said that just when Job J was returning from the kitchen with the jug of wine under his arm. He says, 'We all tend to become marginal, to live on the edge of things. Samm hasn't understood that yet, although she's the most marginal of us all, given her Montagnais heritage. When she learns the point to which she's determined by her redskin past she'll drop the hospital quick.' Samm says, 'In Mattavinie Job J lends me his old books and I'm learning little by little about Pointe-Bleue. It's hard because I'm twenty-five and terribly ignorant.' I say, 'So was Melville, Samm. What was he before then? Less than nothing because his own life was a mystery to him. He didn't know how to structure it, how to make decisions. He was a tenantless body, like yours is at the moment. At some point he had to take things in hand in order to find out who he was. It was no leisurely choice but an emergency. That's the state you have to aim at, where you're forced to become what you already are.' Father says, 'You never become anything. You just die. And you don't even choose where. Sometimes I wonder where all of this is going to lead you, Abel.' I say, 'I don't know, you search, that's all.' Father says, '"Organize", that's the word nowadays.' I say, 'That's never interested me. To organize you have to believe in order. But it doesn't exist, never has. In the final analysis, we're at the same point as Melville: we're eighteen and we don't know what to do with ourselves. I mean, doing with ourselves what others before us did with themselves just doesn't interest us.' Father says, 'Thank you, Abel.' I say, 'I'm not speaking against you, Father. Like the rest of us, you were destined to do what you did. But in your case, it was inside a circle whose circumference consisted of the family, religion and the nation. Your hands were tied and you simply followed where it all led. It's different for us, we've got to find it in ourselves, somewhere among the debris of your world. Do you understand what I'm trying to say?' Father nods his head then points his finger at me. Wine puts him in a fighting mood and easily destroys the image he would have of himself. Before, Jos and I would come sometimes to the house, each carrying a quart of wine. We would set them on this same living room table and Jos would take the corkscrew out of his pocket. He would open both bottles and offer one to Father who would pretend to be watching television. Jos would say, 'You're not Noah, don't worry about getting drunk. Have a drink with us.' Father made us twist his arm but always wound up accepting the bottle. At that point Mother would lock herself in her room. She'd always hated to see us drink, especially Jos who at that time took himself for Stavrogin and threatened to kill either himself or the rest of us. One day he even drew a hatchet from his gabardine suit and sent it sailing into the artificial palm tree in front of the window, cutting the little hanging monkey in two. At first Father would always laugh, especially when Jos, now become Dostoievsky, began to discourse on the horrors of life. Slowly Jos' speech would get to Father and he would rise from his chair and show us the door, always with the same distress-filled words. I found it sad – his self-image crumbling so easily before Jos' slightest trick.

All of that comes back as Father points his finger at me, his cheeks flushed. If he rises from his chair, I'm as good as dead. I can already see the door closing behind me. But instead he looks at Samm who's devouring him with her eyes: he lets his arm fall as though ashamed of having reacted to my provocation. Then he shudders. He says, 'I almost let myself be had again. I'm not on my guard like I once was. Anybody can take me now. Before there was only Jos.' He laughs, happy at having controlled himself at the right moment, just when Samm's face was showing troubled lines. It's for her, moreover, that Father says, 'You know, we come from a long line of warriors who settled on the heights of Trois-Pistoles. My grandfather fought local parish battles for ten years. It's still with us, enough at least for Abel to want to write about it and for me to still not know how to drink. I don't think Melville came at things from that side.' He laughs once more and says, 'You see what it's like to live with Abel. I don't know anything about his friend Melville and here I am wanting to talk about him. It must be contagious.'

Father's pleased with himself. For a moment he reassumed the highest authority. Now he won't say another

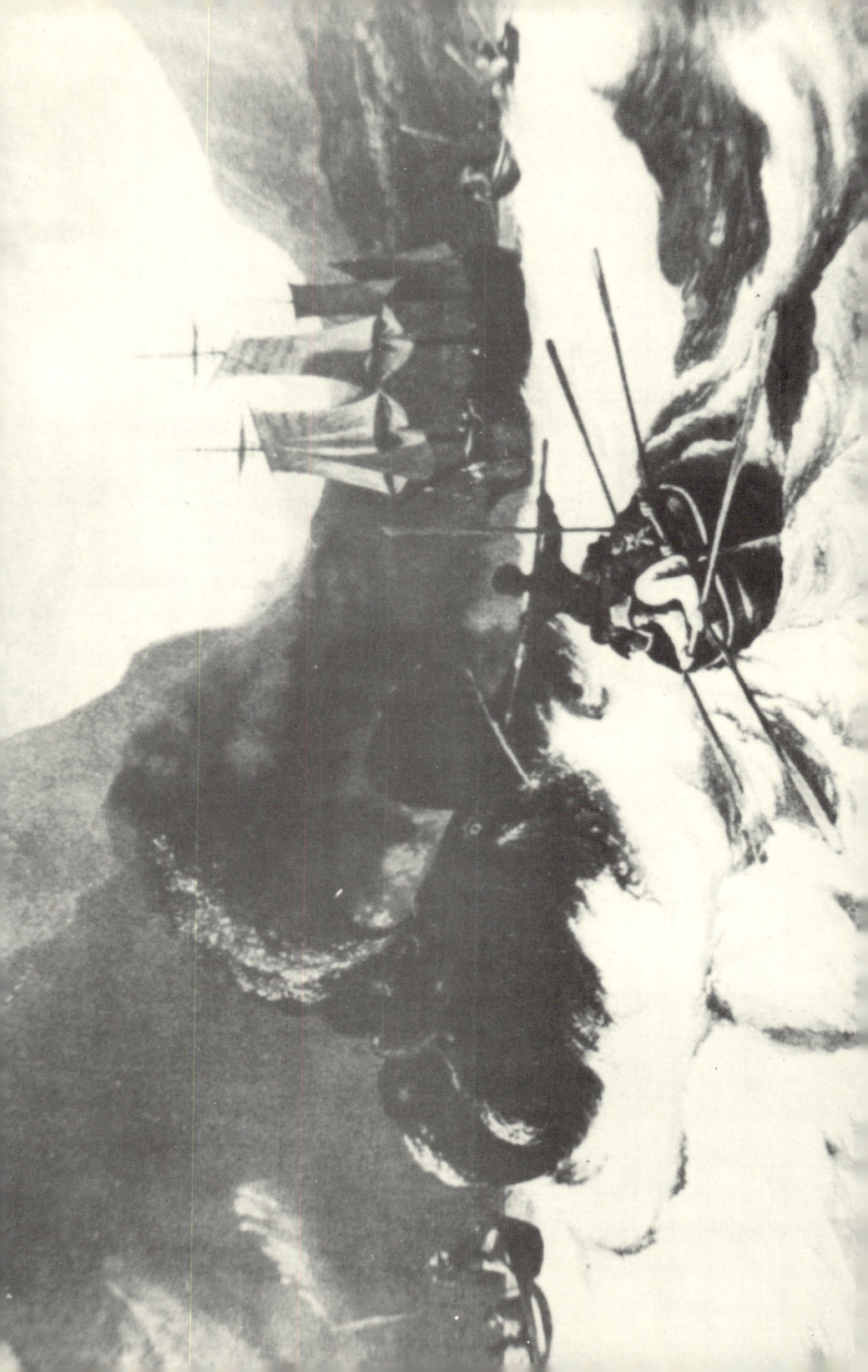

word as he sits in his easy chair with his arms folded. Una says, 'Are there any whales in this house? Is Monsieur Melville a whale? Is that why he's dead, because he was too full of people?' I say, 'There's no whale in the house yet, Una. Later, when you come back to see me. Then it will be a really strange whale, one with a high hat and a long white beard.' Una says, 'You're funny! Whales are blue and their beards are too. I wonder what your book's going to be like if you don't even know that. You should ask Papa-Baby, he knows – whales are just photographs, anyway.'

She takes another sip of my wine and slides down my legs. Then she heads for the door. She says, 'It's time to go, Papa-Baby. If not, the whale can't come.' Job J says, 'We'd have liked you to come with us to Mattavinie, Abel.' Father says, 'It would do you good. Don't worry, I'll look after your manuscript.' Samm says, 'You ought to come with him. Una's pony is a fine beast. You being a horseman, you'd like him.' Father says, 'Me? A horseman? Who told you that?' France says, 'I did. To tell the truth, I don't know if you like horses or not, but when you came to see me in the hospital I figured right away that you must know something about them. My father was something of a horsetrader too.'

Profiting from their unexpected conversation, I rise from my easy chair and go back to the apple-tree wood table. They're going to talk some more while I, energy itself, I'll pick up the work where I left off and not worry about my visitors.

Soon the hall door slams and Father is back beside me, watching me write. He finally says, 'You weren't very nice to them. You might have found a way to refuse their invitation more gently. If you'd gone with them, I'd have gone too. Ponies are hard to turn down.'

But seeing I'm not listening, Father leans his head back; closes his eyes and sinks into a world which I'm forbidden to enter. Softly he says, 'That's it, Abel, that's it, write, poor devil. Write so the whale will come and swallow us.'

10

Spring, 1839: that's where I've gotten to in my sleepless encounter with Melville; I'm able to start up again – even with a certain patience – thanks to Samm and the things she promises. For a while I'll be using her energy together with Melville's and my own as I approach the crux of the work, desiring it, pushing it away. Unsatiated, searching desire is a living force; once satisfied, desire cancels itself out in the illusion of fixity; and furthermore, it's simply to be expected that all things come to grief, destroying creation in their wake.

I wrote 'Spring: 1839'. It's just a date. Perhaps it's only important because of Melville's first voyage as he leaves New England on board the *St. Lawrence* sailing between New York and Liverpool.

Once again I call attention to a coincidence. The first vessel Melville ever set foot on was none other than the *St. Lawrence*. It no doubt belonged to a rich London merchant whose Empire ruled the waves, those leading to Grand Montréal as well as those leading to the pyramids of Egypt – those sea pirates, dealers in spices and glass baubles, all for the Empire.

I imagine that the name *St. Lawrence* must have rung sweetly in their ears; I imagine that, pronouncing the boat's name, they must have had a magical vision of the new world, of Saxon America. I imagine that the crew of the *St. Lawrence* must not have even known that the boat they were sailing on had been named in honour of the mighty river. Moreover, I imagine that they knew nothing of what was lived upon that river's banks, nothing of those little people who for having rebelled once were now living through the throes and pangs of Satan Colborne's repression. I imagine that they hadn't heard nor would ever hear tell of Girod who had recently taken his own life beneath the bridge at Longue-Pointe to keep from falling into the hands either of the *patriotes* or the Red Coats. I imagine they knew nothing of Jean-Olivier Chénier whom the English dragged into the tavern in Saint-Eustache and held down upon a table so that they could have his heart and parade it on stave-point around the village. And I think of the *patriotes* hanged in the Champ de Mars, of Monseigneur Bourget kneeling in the snow with his blood-soaked hand gripping the cross hanging down his chest. I think of all those people of this small country who were murdered and driven into exile with complete indifference while the world turned and ships plowed the ocean to spread commerce's various products throughout the world – and I say to myself that Melville didn't know either. Later, maybe, he knew. Later, when he came to Montréal on his honeymoon with Elizabeth Shaw. Later, when after the failure of *Moby-Dick* he gave conferences and spoke of Roman statuary before the notables of Hochelaga. Later, much later, maybe Melville knew. Probably when the *Acushnet*, the boat he'd embarked upon to hunt the mighty whale, sank in that very same St. Lawrence River.

But in the spring of 1839 Melville was simply crossing the Atlantic on board the *St. Lawrence*. He wasn't yet twenty, he felt ridiculous in his shooting jacket and high-heeled boots and parisian-style pantaloons – slit and buttoned low down the leg! What a strange sailor Melville must have made! And what a lesson he learned from it! Too poor to pass himself off as a bourgeois and just wealthy enough not to belong to the commonality. Why was he going on this trip? He thought he knew:

> I could no longer remain in my room, the house was closing in on me like a shrinking nut, the walls banged against my

Louis-Joseph Papineau addressing the *patriotes*.

Prince's Dock, Liverpool, at the time of Melville's first voyage.

forehead. So, hatless, I took my leave, conscious that only in the infinite air would I discover the space necessary for the unlimited expansion of my life.

But now that the *St. Lawrence* was underway upon the Atlantic none of that carried any weight, it got lost in the wide heave and swell of the mountainous waves:

> Sailors all around me; I listen. When you're my age and look absurd in your dress, you have nothing to say. What Max the Dutchman calls 'soaking it'. He must not realize how right he is where I'm concerned; as I don't even have a monkey jacket, I stay drenched in my flimsy dress.

What fascinates Melville now that the shores have all sunk below the horizon is the feeling of being at the centre of the earth because the ocean abolishes all perspective and makes of the *St. Lawrence* the only universe possible. In Melville's eyes the *St. Lawrence* represents something quite different from a simple cargo ship en route to Liverpool; it becomes the condensed expression of the world at large. All those sailors – where are they from? From America, from Ireland, from Holland, from England, from Denmark: they constitute that transient humanity, the toilers of the sea. A hierarchical world ruled over by Captain Riga whose authority is exercised from a distance. You almost never see Captain Riga: all day long he remains shut up in his cabin, his door closed to commoners. He eats his meals and sleeps there, appearing from time to time on the bridge to stare out upon the emptiness, his face a closed book. He's a kind of almighty god who is both nowhere and everywhere on the ship. He's both the substance and the expression of the law – which fascinates Melville, so that when he turns writer he invents Captain Ahab with his unbounded need for power; likewise Benito Cereno, the symbol of fallen power, terrified by the loss of its attributes and now in the hands of his own creatures; inventing afterwards the equivocal Captain Vere of *Billy*

Budd, the force of the law that secretes its own impotence and produces death. No one was to write about it like Melville. Nobody ever took as far as he the multiple identification of the Captain, a man of power who hates to assume it, leaving its exercise to the chief mate.

The *St. Lawrence's* chief mate was typical enough for Melville to say of him in each book that preferably he has a head smooth as a billiard ball, a lemon-yellow complexion, a broken nose – and he's owl-eyed: 'One would say this is Torquemada. Witch-hunting so as not to have to deal with the witch within himself, so as not to be embarrassed by it.' The watch dog of power, that's what the chief mate is. The man of important jobs who gets his orders and insures their respect on the part of the rest, those sailors come from all over. A bully bunch of mercenaries, outlaws, pariahs, rebels and vagabonds knocking about at sea to keep from getting knocked about on land. And then the bottom of the barrel – the almost always nigger cook – sub-human blackness that doesn't count: 'They wash themselves in their own soup pots and ever murmur Bible verses they've memorized.'

One must understand that in those days black men were looked upon as exceptions. I find two distinct images of them: the first was as retarded beings, as overgrown children, which was why they sang such sad songs even when they were happy. Thus to be hunched over their pots was their rightful place. The other image was less reassuring: it came from the slave trade, from the institution of slavery itself, from all that was known to happen on the boats that brought the black Africans to America. They were packed on board like wild, desperate beasts. Sometimes when they revolted against their despair, they became all the more terrible for having been forced into such submission. They murdered, mutilated, cut off heads. Incredible stories were told about such things, and the nigger slave became a mythical being: he was brutal force, pure cruelty, the incarnation of unforeseeable, underhanded Evil. I imagine that the fact of having one on board ship, relegated to the kitchen, must have had an effect on the crew – like an exorcism.

And I think of what Melville does with all this in *Moby-Dick:* creating Daggoo, the black harpooneer whom he describes in classic fashion, that is, giving him all the attributes of the Negro such as the white man imagined him. Melville's Daggoo stands six feet five and has a lion-like tread; suspended from his ears are two enormous gold hoops; he moves about the ship's deck in glorious pomp. A savage god in every sense of the word. Melville says, 'There was a corporeal humility in looking up at him; and a white man standing before him seemed a white flag come to beg truce of a fortress.' Whenever I read *Moby-Dick* I always get the feeling that Daggoo is going to turn into a killer. I get the same feeling about the *Pequod*'s other harpooners, the red Indian Tashtego and Queequeg, a George Washington cannibalistically developed, in Melville's words. For the Greeks, arms were sacred and only heroes were worthy of carrying them. On the *Pequod,* as we'll see, the weapons belong to the Savages as though they alone were capable of being true warriors. The white man sails the boat but does not belong, as Daggoo, Tashtego and Queequeg do, to the primitive world of war.

Mind you, I don't know why I go into that here since we're still only at Melville's maiden voyage between New York and Liverpool. Write this paragraph off to my excitement. And let us move on to the next.

Melville would not soon forget what he learned before the *St. Lawrence* reached the shores of Great Britain: he was a mere memory himself, and it was to nourish that memory that he went to Liverpool in the first place. If not, why before leaving Albany would he have rummaged around in his father's things to find and carry with him the small guidebook that his begetter had used thirty years previously? Stepping off the *St. Lawrence,* Melville might have thought, 'It's as though I had Father in my vest pocket, a few special pieces of his past, secret things just between the two of us that this small guide-book makes possible.'

That grip of the paternal vise that Melville carried everywhere with him as though it were from Allan Melville that the light must come, from him that knowledge must be gained – to know thyself is first and foremost to solve the mystery of the father. All other knowledge is vain without that. There you have the reason Melville combs Liverpool looking for images of his father, walking where he walked, stopping where he stopped according to the small guide-book. A fruitless search because not much was left of the father's Liverpool that the son could recognize:

> Only things in the process of dying, as I said to Augusta. Vagueness, only vagueness remains as though nothing were sure or definite, not even faces – fluid shapes like the water washing the sides of the moored *St. Lawrence* which I stand looking at from the dock now that I know there's nothing in Liverpool that I could transform along with myself. What misery, what accumulation of poverty, all these people crawling the streets begging for pence, dull eyes in drawn faces, deformed bodies draped in rags, all these babies wailing in the murky society of Liverpool, all these filthy, disreputable streets, row upon row of houses of ill repute, this port and its blackened waters, all these odours, infamy's stench – and all that I am but want no more to be, all that I find of myself everywhere and would wipe out forever. To travel at last like Uncle De Wolf, to enter these foreign countries where there's nothing of me, nothing but the newness of another life. Augusta! If you only knew how bored I am! If you only knew how bored I am still in this Liverpool infested with beggars, swarming with dying, crippled, mutilated souls! That abandoned woman wandering the docks with two whimpering infants clasped to her bosom. That beggar who pursued me back to the *St. Lawrence,* screaming because I had nothing to offer him. Augusta! This

whole overpopulated, repressed crowd of creation! I'm eager for the *St. Lawrence* to cast off with its load of Irish immigrants. They speak of America as a great country where you can forget the famine in Dublin and the waters of the Liffey, now just so much mud. Don't they know they'll find nothing there but their same poor selves – if they don't die, that is, on the way? They'll gather on deck, craning their necks for a glimpse of the promised land. During a storm they'll be driven below into steerage and their slowly rising prayers will be enough to make one feel sick. Misshapen animals sealed off in darkness without water with which to wash, without fire, without anything. The world's spectacle is truly a sad one, my poor Augusta.

Later, Melville adds that, no, Liverpool wasn't quite what he expected. How astonished he was at the all-enveloping gray fog. He says, 'Everything was invested with mystery, more so since as we were disembarking we were startled by the doleful, dismal sound of a great bell tolling regularly. I thought I had never heard so boding a sound; a sound that seemed to speak of judgment and resurrection....'

But not everything that's related in *Redburn* is essential. It was when he'd finally arrived in Liverpool that Melville understood what it meant to be a sailor. It was in strolling around Liverpool that he realized there was little connection between Cousin Guert's naval yarns and the day-to-day reality of a seaman's life:

> Liverpool, it is true, opened my eyes. I understood then that sailors go round the world without once penetrating it, remaining always on the edge of the circle. My comrade Lowry was fascinated by Liverpool; he'd never seen such a 'considerable city' though he'd sailed as far as Madagascar. He was impressed by the lay-out, row upon row of 'considerable houses'. Personally, I would have liked to get at what was being lived inside them. But that's forbidden to ordinary sailors. They must make do with appearances.

When a cargo ship puts in at Liverpool the Queen of England doesn't send her finest carriage to greet it! So what is Liverpool then? Simply a town like so many others in the world, full of hostile people. With Father's guide-book in hand, I merely wanted to repeat his voyage, stopping where he had stopped, eating where he had eaten, seeing what he had seen. But nothing lasts, the Liverpool that Father knew no longer existed; it had given way to another. And if one day my son Malcolm were to make the same trip he'd merely find the same: the world dies and the son cannot remain the son. He becomes the Father or blows his brains out. There is neither past nor future. There is only the bright shining present moment. I was probably alone among us not to understand: the other sailors on the *St. Lawrence* preferred to buy themselves a good time. Around the port it was all arranged for you, and you were going to leave ship in New York poorer than when you boarded it.

But Liverpool is Harry Bolton also, a bosom buddy to chase away the fog of Great Britain. On every one of Melville's voyages there'll be a Harry Bolton, thus I linger here. In the description of him in *Redburn* you've already got Billy Budd, and Queequeg, and Jack Chase, and Long Ghost. In its lyrical accents, Wellingborough Redburn's description of him reminds one of Melville's final work, especially when you read it in the original instead of the often dull French translations. In *Redburn* Melville writes of Harry Bolton:

> He was one of those small, but perfectly formed beings, with curling hair, and silken muscles, who seem to have been born in cocoons. His complexion was a mantling brunette, feminine as a girl's; his feet were small; his hands were white; and his eyes were large, black, and womanly; and, poetry aside, his voice was as the sound of a harp.

When I read *Redburn* for the first time, this description intrigued me: Melville's friends all have something of the feminine about them, in body as in soul. Obviously they're all of royal blood even though they're orphans. What meaning should one give to this constant in Melville's work, this friendship between men, the one considering himself insufficient with respect to the other who represents beauty at its highest? My question would surely seem absurd to Melville; he would answer as he answered in *Redburn* – with a metaphor.

As always, names count, those at least with which Melville baptizes his creatures. What could be clearer than Harry Bolton speaking tenderly to Wellingborough Redburn of his involvement with a certain Lord Lovely? Likewise, the trip that Harry Bolton and Melville take to London, the first disguised behind a thick moustache, the other dressed as a dandy, feminized by his clothes. It all being confirmed by what follows: in London, Harry Bolton plays the dominating male, Melville the young pretty girl who is too naive to see that her friend is mentally unstable and of a suicidal nature. The entire scene, among the best in *Redburn*, is one long series of confused exchanges which, far from making it clear who the characters really are, almost deliberately obscures who and what they are for each other. A dubious sort if there ever was one, wasn't Harry Bolton merely a homosexual who was desperate because his love affair with the enigmatic Lord Lovely had ended? Of course, Melville doesn't say so, and preferred to curtail Redburn's questions as the *St. Lawrence* sailed for home.

On board, of course, was Harry Bolton who had decided to flee old England for the New World. Poor Harry Bolton! He who had pretended to be a sailor's sailor and yet couldn't even climb the rigging, making him the butt of the crew's cruelest jokes. Melville says, 'I pitied this hopeless man who could not go aloft. The fact was, *his nerves could not stand it*; in the course of his courtly career, he had drunk too much strong Mocha coffee and Gunpowder tea, and had smoked altogether too many Havannas.'

BY HERMAN MELVILLE.

REDBURN.

One Volume, 12mo, Muslin, $1 00; *Paper, 75 cents.*

Ships and the sea, and those who plow it, with their belongings on shore—these subjects are identified with Herman Melville's name, for he has most unquestionably made them his own. No writer, not even Marryat himself, has observed them more closely or pictured them more impressively.—*Albion.*

A delightful book. A quiet vein of humor runs through it that will better repay the exploring than many of the veins will gold-digging.—*Courier.*

It is unquestionably a work of genius, and quite as interesting as it is unique; and we know not where a better idea of sailor life can be found than in its pages.—*National Intelligencer.*

As perfect a specimen of the naval yarn as we ever read, and displays much various talent and power. The characters are exceedingly well drawn.—*London Literary Gazette.*

This book is intensely interesting. The great charm of the work is its realness. It seems to be *fact*, word for word. The tale is told simply and without the least pretension; and yet, within its bounds, are flashes of genuine humor, strokes of pure pathos and real and original characters.—*Boston Post.*

The life-like manner in which every event is brought to the reader is astonishing.—*Home Journal.*

This book is in the old vein. It is written for the million, and the million will doubtless be delighted with its racy descriptions of the life of a young sailor.—*Noah's Times and Messenger.*

Redburn is a clever book. * * * All who have read "Omoo" will remember that the author is an adept in the sketching of beautiful originals.—*Blackwood's Magazine.*

The freshness and rich coloring of his writings, with his easy and pointed style, his humor and descriptions of scenery and character, have earned for him the name of the Defoe of the Sea.—*Baltimore American.*

Redburn will prove a most readable book.—*Richmond Whig.*

The style of the book is exceedingly attractive. In our view it has higher merits than any other volume from the same pen.—*Hartford Republican.*

Redburn is no ordinary book. If an imaginary narrative, it is the most life-like, natural fiction since Robinson Crusoe.—*Southern Literary Messenger.*

In the filling up there is a simplicity, an ease, which may win the attention of a child, and there is a reflection which may stir the profoundest depths of manhood.—*Literary World.*

Herman Melville is one of the few who has made a distinct mark on the literature of his time.—*Philadelphia North American.*

The author of this volume needs no commendation. He has already found his audience, and it is not wanting in numbers, in taste, in discrimination. No writer plans better than he; no one uses better materials, or gives them better workmanship; no one puts on a more exquisite finish.—*Worcester Palladium.*

Harper & Brothers, Publishers, New York.

Advertisement announcing Harper's publication of *Redburn*.

In the eyes of the crew, Harry Bolton's saving grace was the fact that every now and then when night came, he would sing in a voice so sweet and feminine as to enchant one. Harry was nothing apart from that. His arrival in New York was pathetic. When Melville leaves him to return to his family in Albany, you're sure there's nothing left for Harry Bolton to do but kill himself.

Yet, finishing *Redburn* you find that that's not what happened. In the final chapter, Melville tells us that several years after the voyage to Liverpool a veteran tar, whom he met by chance in the Pacific, confirmed Harry Bolton's sad end. Shipping out on a whaler because he couldn't find work in New York City, Harry Bolton died a terrible death: during a manoeuvre, he fell over the side and was crushed between the ship's hull and a whale they were flensing.

It's no accident that *Redburn* ends with the death of a friend. In all of his works, Melville does the same thing: after the epiphany comes the world of shadows. For Melville, friendship among men is always guilty, there can be no happy ending. Love between persons of the same sex brings its own punishment: Harry Bolton dies torn to pieces between a whale and a boat's hull; Queequeg drowns; Billy Budd kills Claggart with a single blow and is hanged; in Melville's own life, Nathaniel Hawthorne kept his quiet distance, not knowing how to react to a friendship he didn't understand.

Perhaps this is the first lesson Melville learns from his trip to Liverpool: true fraternity is a fragile and uneasy thing; once found, it tends to fall apart. Nothing's left but sea travel, that baptism which isn't one, in fact, since it merely throws you back upon yourself, putting you in a stagecoach leaving New York City, headed for Albany and your family's world.

11

Melville's first voyage couldn't have made a hero of him: how could that little crossing compare to the odysseys of John De Wolf or Cousin Guert? It was thoroughly banal, of little interest to anybody. Perhaps only to Augusta really. It was she, of course, who opened the door when Melville arrived at Lansingburgh, his voyage already far behind him. Augusta smelled him all over, pretending it was sea odours she was after, even going so far as to ask him for his monkey jacket. Melville had missed Augusta too; she was almost a grown woman now. Of Liverpool, of his adventures with Harry Bolton, he spoke only to her. The others knew nothing; they were satisfied to have the prodigal son home again and ready, apparently, to settle down like the rest of them into a daily routine. Now that his voyage was over, Melville found himself in about the same position as before he left: he was unemployed and his family could ill afford him, there were too many other mouths to feed.

It was towards the end of summer, 1839: Augusta and Melville still went together to sit beneath the big oak in Longmeadow to seek the calm of the rocky red earth which was too close to the mountains to be really fertile but which the patience – and desperate courage – of early settlers had rendered livable. This is something I can understand for knowing Mattavinie where Job J has his farm; it bears a strange resemblance to Melville's Massachusetts: the same configuration of the soil, the same pebble dikes in the form of fences, the same saplings and spruce, stunted because of the solid rock a few inches below the loose earth. After all, it's

New England scene: the Berkshires.

not for nothing that Melville and I understand each other so well: we share the same world, we stand on the same side of things.

What else can one say about Melville's return that isn't already found in the biographies? A word or two about his mother, perhaps. Wearing that long dress that covers her poorly – she's gotten heavier in the last four months, and you can see the lines and the crow's feet now – she'll soon be old; and Melville wonders what she'll do when her children are spread all over like dandelions. And are these children running about the house really his brothers and sisters? Melville's astonished at how his own family have become strangers. So he's ready to do anything, even leave them another time. It was Augusta who showed him the notice published in the Albany newspaper asking for a schoolmaster in the Sikes District. Melville didn't really want to go: 'Teach! What do I have to teach?' But Augusta succeeded in convincing him nonetheless, and Melville said, 'All right, I'll go bury myself there for the winter. At least they won't be able to accuse me of not doing my part for the family.'

I imagine Augusta helping Melville pack his bags. It isn't difficult because he doesn't intend to carry much with him, just what's necessary to get through the winter. And then Melville heads for the Sikes District. Curiously, at one and the same time he's pleased to no longer be at home and happy not to stray too far. His school is in an isolated spot five miles from the village of Greenbush, and the house in which he takes lodgings sits atop a small primeval mountain from which you can see the surrounding countryside – its poverty; its scrawny trees; its fields, deserted now in late autumn; the large white, frozen spaces. Melville says:

> The family with whom I stayed were the embodiment of the Yankee: shrewd, self-reliant, given little to talking but frank when they did. They had nine boys and three girls, five of whom were my students. Mind you, I can't say that I particularly enjoyed teaching. I simply wasn't cut out for it. I've never had much authority. Imagine, then, what it was like in a class in which the majority of the students could have been my brothers and sisters! In truth, I did what I could. One might as well say 'nothing'. The rest of the time I read everything Augusta and Uncle Peter sent me. I was particularly taken with Shakespeare's *Macbeth*.

I know – Melville's biographers claim that Jack Chase introduced him to Shakespeare, and that Melville read him only once he'd returned from the South Seas. Melville himself writes somewhere that before age twenty-five he knew nothing at all, certainly not Shakespeare. But that doesn't mean very much. Who can say where the truth really lies, especially with a man as aged as Melville? Though it's true that

Melville didn't understand Shakespeare's genius till after his second voyage, it's also true that Uncle Peter sent him *Macbeth* sandwiched between three books on teaching. Unless it was Augusta.

Regardless, the probability of such a thing is enough for me: I'm no literary detective and all I wish to do is to speak of Melville. Here are the circumstances under which he read *Macbeth* and what stayed with him:

> I wonder how my students would have reacted had I read them *Macbeth* with a foot propped on my chair and my head turned towards the window. I've no idea what they would have said had I recited the three witches' words:
>
> *The Weird Sisters, hand in hand,*
> *Posters of the sea and land,*
> *Thus do go, about, about,*
> *Thrice to thine, and thrice to mine,*
> *And thrice again, to make up nine.*
> *Peace! the charm's wound up.*
>
> Or Banquo's remark to them: *Are you aught that man may question?* Or had I read them what Lady Macbeth says:
>
> *... Thou wouldst be great;*
> *Art not without ambition, but without*
> *The illness should attend it. What thou wouldst highly,*
> *That wouldst thou holily; wouldst not play false,*
> *And yet wouldst wrongly win. Thou'dst have, great*
>   [*Glamis,*
> *That which cries, 'Thus must thou do,' if thou have it;*
> *And that which rather thou dost fear to do,*
> *Than wishest should be undone. Hie thee hither,*
> *That I may pour my spirits in thine ear,*
> *And chastise with the valour of my tongue*
> *All that impedes thee from the golden round,*
> *Which Fate and metaphysical aid doth seem*
> *To have crowned thee withal.*
>
> Or further:

All our yesterdays have lighted fools
The way to dusty death. Out, out, brief candle!
Life's but a walking shadow, a poor player
That struts and frets his hour upon the stage
And then is heard no more. It is a tale
Told by an idiot, full of sound and fury,
Signifying nothing.

Only the little girl-student Lowry might have understood and have asked for more. Sitting at the back of the class, her long red hair flowing down her shoulders, nibbling her pencil. Sometimes Melville would see her as he strolled along the river bank. She would be fishing with a hazel-branch instead of a pole. She had a proud look as the sun turned her hair into red gold and the breeze heisted her skirts up to her knees. But Melville didn't dare go sit beside her on the felled tree trunk. He followed his course, his nose stuck in *Macbeth* as he read each character's part aloud, changing his voice accordingly. That desire for power and all one must do to gain it, how far one must embrace corruption and evil even to the point of murdering a blameless friend. In *Macbeth* Malcolm says, 'Blunt not the heart, enrage it.' Melville had tacked this phrase on the wall of his room with a few others gleaned from his reading.

In the Sikes District that year winter seemed endless. How could Melville have been happy teaching when what he wanted was to find out who he was and what to make of his life? But no answers were forthcoming; he was still at the same point, his adolescence merely the continuation of his childhood – and, following his father's death, a continuous state of barren unease. How bored Melville must have been in the Sikes District! His biographers don't talk about it but it's easy enough to affirm when the facts are staring you in the face. At twenty, Melville was already up to his ears in solitude with no way of expressing to others what he felt; any such exchange was beyond him.

This feckless life was to last three years; he emerged from it reading Shakespeare, Edgar Poe, Washington Irving plus a whole series of authors who recounted their adventures at sea. I know from Pierre Frédérick that Melville read *Two Years Before The Mast* which was greeted upon publication as a new *Robinson Crusoe*. The work had considerable success all across America. It was just exotic enough, romantic enough, for the sedentary reader to want to put himself in it. Melville too. He was an average adolescent: no ideals, no ambition: 'A man, just a man, that's all I am.' And that's all he could say for himself. The idea of rebelling didn't even enter his mind. Melville the teacher was walled off in gloomy indifference, and was too indulgent towards others, as well as being too self-complacent. His first writings, articles published in the Albany newspapers, were sincere but little else: their style was heavy, and they were, on the whole, too typical of the genre. Melville was nothing as yet, had become nothing yet. At the same age, Flaubert had completed his development; his work, that is, his life, was already behind him, he had abolished the person and put the character in his place. Melville, on the other hand, was still suspended between dream and reality. He says:

> There in that school in the Sikes District, in out of the way Greenbush, twenty years old and trying to make sense out of my life and wondering whether it was possible to stitch a pattern of understanding into my self-perception. I would have liked to speak about it to Augusta. I wrote her a whole stack of letters but didn't always mail them. Upon rereading them, I found them miserable. I couldn't seem to say what I wanted to say, it remained up in the air. I would think of Father and I didn't always understand; I still couldn't accept the fact that he was no longer with us and that, because of it, nothing seemed possible for me. How shall I put it? Sometimes I felt just like Rip Van Winkle. Or imagined that I was Yan Yost Vanderscamp and the black man Pluto, about whom Washington Irving wrote. I had become those two

The celebrated actor David Garrick posing before a bust of Shakespeare.

A group of sailors as seen by Dorg, a nineteenth-century English illustrator.

roustabouts seeking adventure in their small canoe and tempting the Devil by transgressing against all the taboos in Communipaw and leaving its worthy burghers frozen with horror. It's a marvellous story. The best part of it takes place at the Wild Goose tavern where Yan Yost Vanderscamp and old black Pluto frighten the peaceful burghers and make their heads spin with wild tales of buccaneering boarding parties embroidered with every manner of foreign oath. They clink the can with the burghers, pledge them in deep potations, leave lusty drinking songs ringing in their ears, and, to scare them more, fire their pistols at the ceiling. Cunning pirates worthy of Captain Kidd, scouring the seas, real carousers who burn the candle at both ends. While I was lost in that hole of a Sikes District idly leafing through the books on teaching Uncle Peter had sent me, believing little that I read because it was the same sort of stuff that I might have written in the Albany papers: 'We are the heirs of the past, sharing this heritage with all the nations of the West; all tribes, all peoples united in federation to call Adam's strayed children back to Eden's venerable hearth.'

Empty words to mask an empty life. How did Melville keep from throwing in the towel? How was he capable of living in the desert of Albany? Did he deliberately submit to it in order to help his family till his brothers and sisters were grown? I don't know, even Augusta is no help here. All I can say is that in 1840 Melville left his job as schoolmaster and went home to announce his decision to his family: he was going back to sea. Remembering, perhaps, these lines from *Macbeth*: 'The flighty purpose never is o'ertook / Unless the deed go with it.' Could this single sentence of Shakespeare's have made up Melville's mind for him? How to know? I merely see him embracing Augusta, leaving his mother's house and boarding the large canalboat which is to carry him first to New York City, then to New Bedford. There Melville signed on the whaleship *Acushnet* specializing in long hunts in the South

Seas. His voyage was to last nearly four years. Leaving on the *Acushnet* from Fairhaven January 3, 1841, Melville finally returned October 14, 1844. Those forty-five months at sea were to shape the rest of his life, bringing forth the *oeuvre* and its failure. Forty-five months which produced *Moby-Dick* and *Billy Budd* and almost everything in between – amounting to a single tragic story.

12

Father's given up. He just went to bed. As he passed behind me he tapped me lightly on the shoulder, saying again how wrong I was to drive myself like this. I almost answered that, being alone, I had no need to worry about how I was or what might become of me: Judith didn't need me any longer, she was holed up in Daytona Beach with Julien and the two children he'd given her. Even my own characters want nothing to do with me, they're just as happy to be rid of me. Why then should I give a second thought to my life?

So I remain stubbornly at the apple-tree wood table thinking of what I've written up to this point, not trying, however, to get any more out of myself. I'm going to sink into a dream-like state as I always do when I'm like this – so very full of desire.

Thus I imagine myself on the highway running through the Adirondacks at the wheel of an old blood-red Cadillac with big, shiny fins – and with a whale's tooth beside me on the seat. The American border guards pick it up and weigh it in the palms of their hands, pinching it with their thumbs on all sides. They have to think the tooth's hollow.

The radio's turned up as high as it will go; I'm in a trance. That's how it always is when you start out on the hunt; eyes fixed on the miles and miles of narrow highway, your body tensed as you head towards the objective. Mine is simple: to reach Pittsfield, find Arrowhead and interview Melville. I intend to offer him my whale's tooth as a present. I'm sure Melville doesn't have one like it. Old Captain Coffin gave it to me as Job J ate an apple with Blanche on the deck of *The*

Doris. That was three or four years ago, when they were camping on a small rise in front of the gulf. At that time Job J had just begun his research on whales. For Blanche it was too late: she was preparing herself for her fatal end, it being as ineluctable as the end of Sulphur Bottom himself.

The old blood-red Cadillac with its big, shiny fins is rolling and I'm heading through the American countryside and its fugitive scenes which have become one long stream of sea-green light as rain falls all over the continent. It must be mid-October, red-leaf season. Unparalleled rainfall. In spite of it, I roll down my window and breathe what might be sea-air: it tickles my nose.

It must be noon when I get to Arrowhead, now a museum such as those you find all over America. Melville's name is inscribed on a bronze plaque on the door. But ring as I might, no one answers. So I take a seat on the steps – this feeling of being in a haunted house or upon a deserted ship. I've placed my whale's tooth securely upon my knees, stroking it continuously because I've got much on my mind and could easily leave it here.

I must have dozed off. I sleep so little at night now that I catch up whenever I can. All I need do is close my eyes and I'm gone. I don't know if Melville could do as much. I'll ask him when the museum opens. It shouldn't be long. There – what I was waiting for: footsteps on the gravel. I open my eyes to see a small black man coming up the walk. He looks a bit like the rabbit with white gloves and a large dangling gold watch that Lewis Carroll liked to put in his stories. The small black man passes by without noticing me. When he unlocks the door I rise and follow him in. He takes off his hat and hangs it on the rack and trots over to the counter in the middle of the room, taking up his place behind it. Then he opens a large notebook of sorts and immediately buries his nose in it. I place my whale's tooth upon the counter.

I say, 'This tooth is for Monsieur Melville. Could you give it to him? And tell him that I've come from far away to

The Melville Museum at Pittsfield.

Futuristic vision of Pittsfield.

interview him.' He says, 'Interview Mister Melville? Give him a whale's tooth? What's this all about anyway, my friend?' I say, 'It's just a present. May I see him?'

The small black man gives me a cool, not especially friendly look. He says, 'What do you want Mister Melville to do with your whale's tooth? My advice to you is to go back where you came from. Anyway, Mister Melville doesn't live here any more. I'm just his memory, and memory's never much good. Maybe you'd have better luck in New York City. In any case, you'd be doing me a favour if you went to look there.'

I pick up my whale's tooth and go back out the door, leaving it open behind him. New York's not at the end of the world! I've come all the way to Pittsfield, why not head for Manhattan? Once you've made Broadway, the rest is easy. You merely let yourself be carried along by the crowd. It moves you steadily towards the port. It's easy. All you have to do is blink your eyes and you're there. At this time of night I'm sure to find the man I'm looking to interview, with my friend Abraham Sturgeon's small Japanese tape recorder hidden under my coat. Here's the way it takes place now that we're finally here; I'm too tired to shake off my languid dream, so I head towards Melville to catch him before he leaves on the *Acushnet* this third day of January, 1841.

□

Thus, with my coat draped over my arm I stroll along the docks whistling happily as I wait for him to step out of the fog. Soon it will be dawn. Melville will appear then exactly as I've imagined him.

The dockers have got to come first though, and they do, greeting each other with loud, friendly insults and hard slaps on the shoulder. Already there are shouts and the screech and grind of pulleys, and cranes and derricks high in the sky, and huge vibrating motors; already fumes and fuel infest the air; already wide oil slicks are forming upon the water.

Spotting Melville, I advance towards him and say, 'I'm Abel Beauchemin, I've come to interview you. As agreed, I've brought you a whale's tooth. It's nothing special but it's all I had for you to recognize me by. Come this way.'

I lead him to the far end of the wharf after handing him the whale's tooth. He hasn't even looked at it, nor does he seem particularly surprised to see me here. So I take advantage of the fact and lead him to a small cafe across the way. As though by chance, it's called the Spouter-Inn. Melville takes a seat in front of me, then removes his hat and places his cane upon the table; he glances at the wall clock made in the shape of a ship's wheel. I'd like to get rid of the whale's tooth. Now that Melville's seen it, it's served its purpose. At some point I'm going to put it in the basket on the window sill even if I rouse the big cat lying in it, staring with his yellow eyes at the spider hanging motionless in the middle of the window. Melville's looking at nothing.

A true baleen whale.

I say, 'Excuse me for barging into your world like this but I couldn't think of any better way. I knew you still came to the docks and I told myself that it could continue here as well as anywhere else. Don't you agree?' He says, 'What do you want from me?' I say, 'You remind me of Job J's grandfather.' He says, 'You come from Québec, I believe?' I say, 'Not exactly. From the Gaspé, at least where it begins.' He says, 'Do you know that the *Acushnet* sank in the St. Lawrence Gulf?' I say, 'That's one of the reasons I wanted to see you so much. They found the whale's tooth I've brought you in the very spot where the *Acushnet* went down.' He says, 'Do you know that Lizzie and I went to Montréal and Québec on our honeymoon?' I say, 'Yes, of course. That's the second reason I've dreamed my way to you. My country is very tiny, you see, and we don't often get visitors the likes of you.'

I look at Melville – there's much more than mere distance between us. It won't be easy to overcome. To keep from thinking about it, I ask for red wine. A full bottle that Melville and I begin to drink. After half a bottle nothing has changed: Melville's still staring off into space and I'm still sitting here like a dope.

I say, 'Excuse me but I don't seem to be able to tell you what seemed so clear to me on my way here. Now that you're here in front of me, I'm a little lost in my dream. I don't want to waste your time.'

He pours himself another glass of wine and downs it in one swallow. The cane rolls on the table when he sets his glass down. I look at his hands: they don't look like the hands of a whale fisherman. The rest, yes – large square shoulders, a broad chest, strong thighs. A build which says he'll live to be a hundred. But maybe hands die first, maybe they wear out before the rest. To hide my distress, I turn my face towards the window and the big cat lying on the whale's tooth.

I say, 'Don't worry about me. What's important is that I listen to you.' He says, 'It doesn't help make things any clearer.' I say, 'That's not why I asked to see you.'

He raises his hand to his neck and massages it with small, round strokes. His hair is totally white and must feel like silk. He takes a thin cigar from his pocket and offers it to me. He says, 'Take it. I've others.' I shiver when Melville's fingers touch mine. Such heat, how is it possible? I strike a match on the bottom of my chair and hold it out to Melville. He draws on the thin cigar, the match flame swells and casts shadows on his face. Melville's eyes are much grayer than I thought. He says, 'I'm afraid you're in for a disappointment, poor friend. It's not your fault. You simply don't know that you can't expect anything from somebody whose only goal is the supreme discretion of strolling along the docks of Harlem even though they don't exist any longer. Go back to Gaspé, you'll be fine there. And give old Captain Coffin my greetings. Sulphur Bottom was quite a whale too.'

He downs another glass of wine. His lower lip trembles, his eyes merely two dark spots upon his face. He says, 'In any case, it's late and I must be going. Lizzie's not as patient as before. Mind you, I don't wish to displease you. You've come this long way for me and you're the first to have undertaken such a trip since my death. I owe you that, at least, if nothing else. But you must understand that I'm in an uncomfortable position, I'm rather badly placed to satisfy your desire. It's one of the consequences of death: it deprives you of the images you entertained of yourself, but gives you none with which to replace them. There, I believe I've said most of what I have to say. I really must go.' I say, 'May I come with you?' He says, 'We see no one now, you know. Lizzie's willing; it's I who generally refuse. She'll be quite surprised.'

I leave all the money I have on the table and follow Melville to the door. Just before turning the knob he stops and stares at the big cat asleep in the basket on the window sill. He says, 'My whale's tooth. I was about to forget my whale's tooth.'

The big cat allows himself to be picked up and set to one side. He stretches, his claws scratch the wood. With two paws placed firmly on the basket handle, he waits for us to take the whale's tooth so he can lie down once again. Melville unbuttons his coat. Beneath it, the tooth protrudes slightly at the stomach. I close the door behind us and we walk off into the night side by side down the deserted wharves; all is quiet except for the tapping of the cane on the pavement. Melville takes my arm by way of asking me not to walk too fast. He's quite right – night's eternal return, no hurry. Anyway, a few steps and we're there, Melville and I, in the house he bought in the heart of New York City when, after thirteen years of life in the country, he sold Arrowhead. That was in March 1863, long after the *Acushnet,* long after the lengthy journey to New Bedford and Nantucket, at a time when the Melvillian countryside lay in ruin.

Melville leads me into a sort of drawing room situated at the far end of the hall, then he disappears. I wait for him, seated upon a small chair covered in purple velvet. I recognize the geraniums and the red roses in the window, as well as

New Bedford in the middle of the nineteenth century.

the photographs framed in black on the walls. I realize now for the first time that no one in them is smiling, neither Melville nor his son Malcolm, not Lizzie, not Augusta. Their expressions are vacant.

I turn my eyes away. Now I see only boats. I recognize the *United States*, a man-of-war Melville served on during his return from the South Seas. But I don't see either the *Acushnet* or the *St. Lawrence*. On the other hand there is that lovely scene of New Bedford as it was at the time when Melville became a sailor. The docks are so full of goods you get the impression that the ships are mired in a sea of barrels and casks. I sit wondering what all that whale oil must have smelled like when suddenly exposed to the sun.

Melville returns to the drawing room at last. He sits down on the love seat facing my chair. His eyes run rapidly around the room without settling on anything in particular. He says, 'I brought you into this room because it's the only one that hasn't been disturbed by this our final move. Elsewhere in the house things are already packed up. Here all that's missing is my small collection of old travel books. Have you read Captain Cook?' I say, 'No, not really.' He says, 'Or Vancouver?' I say, 'Not him either.' He says, 'Or Bougainville?'

I say, 'No. But I'm familiar with La Pérouse and Kotzebue. And with the life of Captain Nepos.' He says, 'Now, there you're in ancient history. Captain Nepos doesn't have very much to do with whales. He was after other game. He was merely a fighter who lived by ruse. He would catapult baskets full of snakes onto the decks of enemy vessels. He wasn't really an explorer. He probably didn't even like water very much. He died in bed, poisoned, I believe. But as for Cook and Bougainville – we'll come back to them. One can't navigate the South Seas without them. And that's what you intend to do, isn't it?'

Thus, he understood before I could tell him. Maybe he knew it the moment I accosted him on the docks of Harlem. That's why he spoke of Captain Cook and of Nepos' ruses. For me to get used to the dream and all it will bring in its wake.

I look at him again. He seems less old since we left the port. If his beard weren't completely white, I could easily believe he was a man in the prime of life. His eyes are bright with malice. I'd like him to speak to me right away about Bougainville and Captain Cook. As I tell him so, he raises a finger to his lips. Footsteps in the hallway. Then Lizzie appears; she is wearing a long black dress closed at the neck by a gold brooch. She smiles at me. She says, 'You resemble Nathaniel Hawthorne when we knew him at Pittsfield. Can it be you, come back at last from old England? Herman said nothing about your visit.'

She sits beside Melville on the love seat. Where did he pull the whale's tooth out of? He shows it to Lizzie, explaining to her who I am and why I've come. Lizzie's face hardens, fleeting but intense hostility appearing in it. She says, 'Herman, hadn't you promised never to leave me again? This young man is perfectly capable of travelling alone.' He says, 'It won't prevent you from going to our sister Fanny's as planned. I won't be away long. A few months at most. Afterwards it shall truly be over.' She says, 'Weren't we supposed to go to Arrowhead next week. Since our good Allan moved in, it doesn't seem the same house we lived in. In any case, it wasn't at all the same house this spring.'

Melville shrugs his shoulders. Lizzie says, 'Won't you at least drink something before you go? And I want Nathaniel to tell us all about his long stay in old England.' Melville says, 'We won't have time for that. Nathaniel will tell us about it later.' Lizzie says, 'As you wish, Herman. I'll go to sleep then. Don't forget to close the door well when you leave. Last time you left it open.'

Melville and I are alone once again. He seems happy. For the first time I see his white teeth between his lips. He says, 'I was afraid it would be more difficult. Poor Lizzie! Isn't it strange, her mistaking you for Nathaniel Hawthorne? But it isn't such a bad idea, I think from now on that's what I shall call you. I'll feel then that we belong to the same generation. It will simplify many things. Come.'

We climb a long staircase that leads to a hallway. We pass many closed doors as we thread our way through a line of enormous trunks. We arrive at a door that is open a few inches. Melville pushes it with his foot and we enter what must be his study. There is an iron cot next to the window. It was Melville's death bed. On the table a long quill pen is still standing in an inkwell. Beside it lies a large white sheet of paper upon which are written three lines:

> But, crying out in death's eclipse,
> When rainbow none his eyes might see,
> Enlarged the margin for despair –

I don't dare look at anything else. All I notice are Melville's feet moving about in the room. He says, 'It's not so tragic. You'll see many others. Come help me here.'

Melville wants to move a trunk that's blocking the closet door. I grab the large leather handle with both hands. The trunk is very heavy. He says, 'There is what I leave the world, this simple trunk which no one shall even think to open, perhaps. *Billy Budd* is in it on the very bottom. I want them to find it only at the end, only once the rest shall have been finally used up.' He laughs. Then he says, 'I might have chosen another mania, don't you think, Nathaniel?'

He said 'Nathaniel' in a strange voice. It must have been that way between him and Hawthorne at Pittsfield. I smile, aware that something very important has just happened to me. There is reciprocity between us now, all the constraints have finally disappeared, swept away by the magic of the name with which Melville has baptized me. I feel at one with him now, words seem unnecessary between us.

Melville rummages in the closet and comes up with two monkey jackets, one green, the other brown. He says, 'We'll need these where we're going. Take the brown one, I prefer the green. I wore it on all my trips. The brown jacket is a gift from Hawthorne. It's got two big inside pockets.'

Hawthorne's monkey jacket is a bit large for me but I imagine that with a sweater underneath it won't show. Melville says, 'Now that we've got the basic equipment, let's go, shall we? It takes quite a few hours to get to New Bedford from here.'

Letting me pass in front of him, he closes the door to his study. Then he rests his hand on my shoulder and we go back down the long flight of stairs. Melville's eyes have changed since we put on our monkey jackets. They're oddly brilliant. I have the feeling that if I were to stare into them for too long they would run me through. I think about the Golem of Prague, that magnificently animated figure, and say to myself that that is what Melville has become. All men's eyes become the eyes of God if you think they are the eyes of God, said Don Benito Cereno. Melville says, 'No doubt. But we mustn't miss the stagecoach. There's only one we can catch in this dream. Get a move on, Nathaniel.'

■

If it weren't for the cobblestones under our wheels, I'd say there wasn't much difference between our stagecoach and a train. We're just as comfortable. Melville and I are the only passengers. We're sitting side by side, though I suggested a different arrangement. He refused, I think, because of his eyes; he didn't want them to make me uncomfortable. Melville's eyes are ablaze; they became so the moment the horses took their first step. His face has changed completely. Melville is sitting upright, his elbow placed on the arm rest. He's smoking one of his countless Mexican cigars.

I make myself as small as possible beside him, my left leg slung over my right. I look out the glass in the stagecoach door. I see the port in Harlem far off behind us and the silhouetted ships, and the lamps like will-o'-the-wisps along the docks. Soon we'll be on the road that runs along the ocean into New Bedford. But we're not likely to see much through this foggy curtain that fell between us and the rest of the world the moment we left New York. So we'll manage to get some sleep. Afterwards, Melville will light a new cigar, put his large hand on my knee so I'll feel more at ease, and say, 'What would you like us to talk about? We won't reach New Bedford for a long while yet.'

I fill my pipe with Hawthorne's tobacco and strike a match on my shoe. We're crossing a small bridge now, we can hear the horses' hooves on the wood. I glance at the window pane. All I see is the inside of the coach. I say, 'We're fine the way we are, I think. Why do we need to speak?' Melville says, 'Perhaps you're right, Nathaniel.'

He rests his head on the back of the seat and closes his eyes. I won't disturb him. I'm going to do as he and stick my hands in my jacket pockets. It's curious riding in a stagecoach: when you close your eyes you get the feeling you're travelling at breakneck speed. Also, it's as though you were moving out of yourself, as though that other body in you were being projected into space. I allow mine to leave the stagecoach entirely. It returns to New York City and floats above Bleecker Street just like the ghost of Doctor Sax the time that Kerouac and I were strolling along Beaulieu Street towards the murky-brown Potomac.

Everything is quiet now, which is fine with me. I feel tranquil, I'm simply happy to be here in this stagecoach with Melville on the way to New Bedford.

When the stagecoach stops we look once again out the window. On our left tiny points of light stipple the darkness. It must be Boston where old Major Melville is still on the prowl – he's wearing his knee breeches and his tri-cornered hat, and his cheeks are puffed up with air with which to keep dying fires alive. The driver opens the door. He says, 'It won't be long, gentlemen. We're just changing horses. One of ours bloodied a hoof on some stones. He lost his shoe.' As they unhitch them, the horses shudder and shake their heads – that slobber hanging from their lips. Melville and I still are not interested in speaking. The two worn-out horses must be in the stable with their noses stuck greedily in the feedbag. Their replacements are snorting and champing at the bit. The driver rubs and pats their noses before removing the brakes from the wheels. The whip cracks. The stagecoach takes off with a jolt. It's the middle of the night. Rain begins to fall. I glance once more out the stagecoach window. We're already in New Bedford, the capital of the whaling industry. You can smell it; with all the barrels on the docks and those fabulous three-masters rocking gently on the waves, you feel submerged in oil.

Fortunately, I'm not alone in my excitement: Melville can hardly keep still. And it's time we arrived in New Bedford. After the silence inside the stagecoach, a little excitement's not at all unwelcome. New Bedford fever takes hold of us; the town's so bright beneath that big red eye of a moon staring down on us.

Melville doesn't even wait for the horses to come to a full stop. He opens the stagecoach door. He says, 'Come, Nathaniel. I'm going to show you New Bedford. It's exactly

The myth of Jonah as seen by an ancient illustrator.

as it was when I sailed on the *Acushnet* that first trip.'

I jump down out of the stagecoach, landing at Melville's side. He takes my arm and leads me along streets full of coaches and wagons and tall sailors with lined, weathered faces and shiny white teeth. Melville says, 'It was night when I arrived in New Bedford for the first time. It was just as it is now – cloudy, dark and cold. Since I had little money, I walked the streets for a long while looking for lodgings. In those days boats for Nantucket were rare, and I missed the last packet leaving for there. So I had a night and a day and another night to spend in town before I could get aboard one. But look, Nathaniel, we've arrived too late also, the packet is already under way.'

Because of the sunshine I shield my eyes so I can see what Melville wants to show me: far off in the distance I see something that could be a packet boat. It's about as big as a sardine can and is rolling slowly on the horizon. I grimace. Melville says, 'Now, now, Nathaniel. Don't be disappointed. In New Bedford we'll find things to help us pass the time till the packet comes back. Let's go.'

How could I resist? To tell the truth, I don't want to. Nantucket will be waiting for us when we arrive. So I fall in step with Melville, keeping my eyes wide open so I won't miss anything of this New Bedford through which we move as though through so much hot butter: all these Atlantic coast towns look alike with their squat buildings, their houses lined like sheep along zigzagging streets that funnel you into the port and its docks dark with people. Melville and I have to elbow our way to the Spouter-Inn.

Ever since *Moby-Dick* the Spouter-Inn in New Bedford is famous, as it is elsewhere in the world. There's a Spouter-Inn in New York City, another in Dublin, another in Halifax, another in Amsterdam. In Bombay there are two, just as there are in Cape Horn. But New Bedford's Spouter-Inn is the authentic one. The reason is simple: it's because of the large oil painting that you can't miss as you enter the place. In Mattavinie, France is making me a fine reproduction of it. Like me, when she read *Moby-Dick* she was fascinated by that besmoked, defaced depiction of Cape Horn in a great hurricane. You're presented a half-foundered ship weltering there with its three dismantled masts alone visible, and an exasperated whale, purposing to spring clean over the craft, is in the enormous act of impaling himself upon the three mast-heads. Melville says, 'It's rather impressive, isn't it –

such an unaccountable mass of shade and shadow – don't you find?'

The wall opposite the large painting is hung all over with a heathenish array of monstrous clubs and spears. Some are thickly set with glittering teeth resembling ivory saws; others are tufted with knots of human hair. Then Melville calls my attention to a particularly strange whaling lance: it is sickle-shaped with a vast sweeping handle. He says, 'With that lance Nathan Swain killed fifteen whales between a sunrise and a sunset. One day, in the Java Sea, he flung it into a whale that ran away with it, not to be slain till years afterwards off the Cape of Blanco. The iron had entered nigh the tail, and, like a restless needle, travelled full forty feet through the blubber and at last was found embedded in the hump.'

But we can't stay in the hall all night. So we go through the low archway – cut through what in old times must have been a great central chimney with fireplaces all round – and enter the public room where on a bench presides old Peter Coffin. I notice the long, low, shelf-like table covered with cracked glass cases filled with dusty rarities gathered from the world's remotest nooks. All that's missing is the whale's tooth I gave to Monsieur Melville in New York City so that he'd recognize me. When I tell him that he unbuttons his monkey jacket, reaches into the big inside pocket and comes up with the very same tooth, which he places on the table between two cases full of bones. As he does so I look at the bar – a rude attempt at a Right Whale's head. Melville says, 'How's business, Peter Coffin?' Old Peter Coffin says, 'If it's a room you're wanting, why I ain't got a bed left.' Melville says, 'You've done this to me before, Peter Coffin.' Old Peter Coffin says, 'But avast, you haint no objections to sharing a savage harpooneer's blanket, have ye, or I can accommodate ye.' Melville says, 'Just as before, Peter Coffin. Just as before! But this time I'm with my friend Nathaniel. We won't be given the business as easily as that.' Old Peter Coffin says, 'So long as you pay me, the rest is another man's matter, not my own.' Melville says, 'Well, rather than wander –' Old Peter Coffin says, 'All right; take a seat. Supper's the thing to get you ready for bed. It'll be ready directly.'

He disappears behind a door. Melville says, 'Dumplings, Nathaniel. Dumplings with meat and potatoes. You'll see, there's nothing better. Nobody serves dumplings as good as Peter Coffin's.'

They're not bad, as a matter of fact, they're just what your stomach needs. Then I say, 'We should get down to business, Monsieur Melville.' He says, 'Soon, Nathaniel. Let's finish our dumplings first.'

But I'm already nodding out. I say, 'Perhaps we could go to sleep?' Melville says, 'With the savage harpooneer?' I say, 'With the savage harpooneer.' He says, 'In that case, we might stay up a bit longer. No man prefers to sleep two in a bed. In fact, one would a good deal rather not sleep with his own brother. I imagine what it must be sleeping three in a bed. I suggest we'd be better to try those wide benches.'

I say nothing; Melville doesn't recall having had the same idea when he came to sail on the *Acushnet*; it's stayed in his mind. Old Peter Coffin has fun with him, saying 'So you

wish to bed down on the bench? Well, between it and the savage harpooneer, I'm sure I know which I'd choose. I'm sorry, I still can't spare ye a tablecloth for a mattress; it'd be almost as good as your Canadian gannet feathers.' I say, 'Don't go stirring up Canada any more, Peter Coffin. We've had enough of that. Show us to our room.'

Old Peter Coffin winks at me, then starts off with a candle in his hand. We follow him to the room. Upon entering, Melville says 'Cold as a clam!' I glance around the room; besides the bedstead and centre table, I see only a rude shelf and a paper fireboard representing a man striking a whale. Then I notice a hammock lashed up and tossed upon the floor in one corner, and a large seaman's bag which must belong to the savage harpooneer.

But I don't want to think about that yet. Later, we'll see. For the moment all that's on my mind is climbing into bed where I'll fill my pipe and wait for Melville to fall asleep. It won't take long.

I look at him; it's ridiculous, but I'd like to throw myself in his arms and roll around with him in this huge bed, and cry my heart out; I'd ask him to let us stay here and forget about Nantucket and the *Acushnet*, even to forgo the trip to the South Seas he agreed to take with me because he knows I love him, because he knows that I'm at one and the same time Hawthorne and his son Malcolm, and Jack Chase, and Billy Budd, and Clarel, all that's left, that is, of imagination for him after all these years of solitude. I'd like to press myself against him, give him my warmth so he'd have the courage to stay up with me, the courage to wait for the savage harpooneer and never think of his son Malcolm again. He's lying on his side, his eyes closed – doubtless so as not to see Queequeg's bag in the corner of the room. I don't dare touch him. I have the feeling that if I did, he would crumble. All my trouble for nothing. I'd have to get back into the old blood-red Cadillac with the big, shiny fins that is waiting by the Harlem docks and return to Québec. I say, 'Are you asleep,

Monsieur Melville?' He doesn't answer. I can hardly hear him breathing. I reach for my pipe on the floor beside the bed. I intend to fill it again and light it, then suckle it like a mother's breast. I say, 'Sleep, Monsieur Melville. I'll be the one to stay awake in this dream.'

☐

Then the savage harpooneer enters the room. I watch as he kneels and digs into his seaman's bag. Rising and coming towards the bed, he's as surprised as I am to find me next to Melville. I raise a finger to my lips to prevent one of those guttural cries of Queequeg's that frightened Melville so much the last time. He smiles at me, visibly happy at having become my accomplice so easily. Queequeg is a fine, strapping man, broad-shouldered and with beautifully developed muscles; his yellowish skin is covered with tattoos; and his roving black eyes, sparkling with mischief, stare straight at me.

The tomahawk doesn't scare me: the Montagnais of Pointe-Bleue have equally efficient ones. And then, one way or another, we all wind up getting scalped. So Queequeg's tomahawk doesn't faze me. Looking at him again, I even feel closer to him because of my miscreant nature, which explains why I'm drawn to marginal types and crackpots. I can recognize myself even from a distance. And what I recognize as I look at Queequeg has nothing to do with Melville's troubled shudders when he saw him for the first time.

Queequeg strips naked and crawls into bed between Melville and me. Now it's he who is looking at me – attentively, ignoring Melville's snores. We don't speak. Sleeping with a man has always excited me, I don't know why. It doesn't give off the same sensuality nor does it offer the same attraction as a woman's body. It always makes me extremely vulnerable and leaves me feeling warm inside. My very skin feels different, becoming a thousand times more sensitive. It was a great discovery for me to learn this when Antonin, Job J and I lived in the apartment house on the rue St-Denis. I imagine that if I had become a sailor, it would have been for that reason. Because of his upbringing, I doubt that Melville would ever be able to accept that two men, full of love for each other, should feel the need to offer themselves totally to each other.

I don't know how I'm going to broach the subject with Melville when the time comes. He's never spoken about it except here and there in his novels, and in the extraordinary love letters that make up his correspondence with Hawthorne. However, at the period of Melville's trip on the *Acushnet,* male friendship of this type was a common occurrence. To go on a four-year voyage with only a band of vigorous men for company – hearty, well-built types little given to solitude – was enough to turn your head after a while. I can imagine what it must have been like – beautiful muscular bodies, sun-darkened skin save for strangely white buttocks, male members hard in the dark, all the more prodigious and threatening since there was a moral code forcing you to see this proposal of beauty as a most hideous vice. I couldn't have. I mean to say, I couldn't have lived for long with all those men without my hands starting to roam, and widely – the wafting musky odours, how provocative it must have been!

Such are my thoughts as Queequeg sits staring at me. In no time at all I explain to him what I'm doing in the room and why I'm making the trip with Melville this time. Queequeg says nothing as I speak. He merely nods as though agreeing. Soon I'll ask him to let me touch him, to let me run my fingers over his tattoos. It's curious. Somehow I feel that Queequeg's memory is encrusted in his skin. Entirely in relief from head to toe. I touch Queequeg's body ever so lightly with my open hand, meeting the richness of the red

world, its unbelievable precision, its unparalleled fullness.

Queequeg and I remain lying on our backs, our bodies so close together that I can feel the blood pulsing in his veins. He continues to smile at me, flashing his beautiful white teeth. What a fascinating double watch we're standing – it ends when I fall asleep to dream of soft moist lips upon mine and of two strong thighs closed tightly around my sex.

When I awake Queequeg is sound asleep. My head is resting on his left arm. Melville has hold of his other. There was some truth then in what Melville wrote in *Moby-Dick*: 'You had almost thought I had been his wife.' But now there are two of us in that role, lying on opposite sides of him: the light streaming in the window makes his stark naked body seem even more imposing than it appeared last night; it's indefinably soft, discreet even, despite that member as stiff as a pike-staff.

I don't dare wake Queequeg. Melville opens his eyes, he gives me a wink. Together we free ourselves from Queequeg and climb out of bed. Queequeg groans; he brings his arms together and rolls over on his stomach. All the while Melville and I continue to dress. Melville says, 'Let him sleep. He will undoubtedly join us on the docks.'

We go out of the room leaving Queequeg still fast asleep. After a hearty breakfast we head down to the docks and go aboard the packet boat, on our way to Nantucket at last. It's still the third day of January, the day Melville and I are to leave for the South Seas.

☐

Melville says, 'In olden times an eagle, like a demi-god, appeared high above the New England coast. It was an eagle such as had never before been seen, being completely white, and guided by preternaturally wide and mighty wings. His coming foretold strange occurrences in the land. And, indeed, there was not long to wait; for the eagle then swooped down upon the coast, leaving a trail of fire behind him. When he climbed again he was holding an infant Indian in his talons, his direction due east. The infant was the only child of a mighty sagamore, who, with his tribesmen, resolved to follow in the same direction. Setting out in their canoes, they rowed furiously. Off upon a fantastic voyage that saw many red-men die before they should reach Nantucket. This semi-divine eagle was circling above the island; nay, the fiercest arrows could not fell him, for it was written they should not. So they began to search for the infant. Their search lasted three full days and three full nights, ending upon the discovery of a small ivory casket, empty but for the skeleton of the sagamore's male-child. The wise-men saw this as a sign: the tribe must remove to Nantucket, there to be its first inhabitants. Thus Nantucket's birth according to the red-man. Europeans landed there for the first time in 1602, and found half a million red-men upon the island. But the white man's arrival changed everything. As history has taught us, the vehicle of change was simple shady dealing – the Coffins, the Husseys and the Starbucks managed to fleece the red-men out of their land for a few dollars. The sagamores of Nantucket didn't understand the significance of the documents they were being asked to sign. When, finally, they did, it was too late. Dispossessed like the Mohawks in Massachusetts, like the Flatheads in Kansas, like the Miami in Missouri. There you have my Tashtego's origins.'

I listen to Melville as the packet boat plows towards Nantucket. Since we cast off, Melville has remained still beside me. We're leaning over the rail between two life boats, out of sight of the tourists, their cameras clicking incessantly as they screech like het up sea gulls.

Melville says, 'You know, I invented little. When you know how to read, it's hardly worth the trouble. In any case, you know as well as I that the Starbucks were the first family to build a house on Nantucket, the first settlers. That is what is so strange about Nantucket's beginning – settled by Eastern Quakers, come to work the land. No doubt giving rise to the old legend which has it that the hostile climate made the land on the island the way it is today. Originally, Nantucket is supposed to have been a gigantic clam. Because of the cold, the clam burrowed into the earth; thus Nantucket's aspect, making you think of an enormous shell rising out of the water. They say, too, that Nantucket resembles a fish, but that's of recent invention. In the days of the Starbucks, one didn't go so far to fetch his symbolism. Life was a homier affair, and one lived in expectancy, as it were, of what would come. It came in 1664 when a new proclamation of the King of England forced the colonists on Nantucket to pay a tribute: four barrels of cod to be delivered annually to the City of New York. Creating, so it seems, such a taste among our islanders for fishing that in 1672 Captain John Gardner was mandated by the island's owners to begin to fish commercially for cod. Doubtless explaining why they didn't go after the whale right away. It's true that, from time to time, whites and red-men went out together after a whale spotted off Nantucket, but those were exceptional cases: whale fishery didn't become an industry there until the beginning of the eighteenth century. And even then they weren't able to go far out after them. After a successful strike, they came immediately back to port to deposit it on the beach before extracting its oil. But since they left the carcasses behind, it seems that the strong east winds carried such a stench into Nantucket that the islanders hid in their houses behind locked doors and boarded up windows. But whale fishery continued to grow. In 1730 Nantucketers were in every ocean in pursuit of every sort of whale. A Starbuck even had the honour of being the first American to export whale oil to England. But there weren't many red-men left on the island. An epidemic, occurring in the winter of 1764, reduced their number to fewer than a hundred. No one knows what caused the epidemic nor why it attacked only the red-men. Most of the survivors went far away from the sea to forget what they had been through. My Tashtego came from all this, too.'

After that, Melville falls silent, the better perhaps to let Nantucket come to us. We can already see the port through the fog. I'm thinking about Queequeg whom we haven't seen since morning. Maybe he stayed in New Bedford in that inn with the window giving on the port. Maybe he's still sitting in front of his wooden idol intoning Rokovoko's holy words with no memory of what took place between us – that searing emotion, the beauty of his body lying next to mine.

Melville and I are the first to leave the boat, leaving behind tourists and old sea-dogs with their toothless smiles. Drawn towards the dream, Melville is really walking too fast. I, however, wish only to take in my surroundings; I recognize everything even if I've never been here before – these old streets, this whole arrangement designed to hold time fast in the settlers' rough stones; this wood eaten by salt; the stiff east wind; this brown earth that was once the red-man's.

So here we are heading through Nantucket's streets, Melville moving like a bat out of hell, I struggling to keep up. I say, 'Let's stop a moment. If we continue at this pace, we'll drop dead in our tracks at some point and never see the *Acushnet* at all.' Melville laughs loudly, then stops. He reaches in the inside pocket of his monkey jacket and comes up with a thin Mexican cigar. Sweat is beading his forehead. He points across the street to Mitchell's Book Corner. He says, 'I must go meet Queequeg. I don't think it would do for Captain Ahab to see you right away. Might I suggest that you speak a while with Master Henry Mitchell Havemeyer. Tell him I sent you. He'll take you into the back room and make you privy to all he's got and knows on whale fishery. We shall see each other again at the Whaling Museum at nightfall. Be there. I shall come with Queequeg and a proper contract to sign you on the *Acushnet*.'

In the watchtower – Nantucket.

He smiles. I don't dare say what I'm thinking – that Nantucket wouldn't be much without him. A dwindling, fading dream good for little more than to be stared at randomly through a camera's indifferent eye. I say, 'Don't leave me behind.' His hand rests on my shoulder as we cross the street. I say, 'You're right, of course. I'll truly be waiting for you then at the Whale Museum at nightfall. We'll go eat a cod-chowder at Hosea Hussey's, then go aboard ship. After that, we won't ever again be separated.'

He pats me on the shoulder with his large hand, offers me a cigar, then turns on his heel and walks off. I lean against the front of Mitchell's Book Corner and watch as he moves down the street with long, impatient strides. Then I enter Master Henry Mitchell Havemeyer's shop. He is seated behind an old pine counter. The first thing I notice is his sparsely furnished crown, and my thoughts return straightaway to Pittsfield: either my eyes are playing tricks on me or, there sitting right in front of me is the small black man I met at the Melville Museum – the small rabbit Monsieur Lewis Carroll liked to put in his stories, wearing glasses this time, square ones that look as though they were made out of Meerschaum. Master Henry Mitchell Havemeyer says, 'May I help you?' He closes the book he's reading, as well as the notebook in which he no doubt notes everything concerning whale fishery. Then he caps his pen and places it next to the notebook. Only once all of that is done does he rise, and then with almost exaggerated slowness. Fascinated, I don't even think of answering him; I watch him straighten up, expecting to hear his bones crack. When he addresses me a second time, I say, 'Monsieur Melville suggested I come here. We just got off the boat from New Bedford and Monsieur Melville preferred that I not follow him to see Captain Ahab.' He says, 'You thinking of signing on, too?' I say, 'Tonight we should be on our way to the South Seas.'

He lifts the board to step over to my side of the counter. He takes my hands in his. I glance at the shelves full of books. As I raise a hand to take one down, Master Henry Mitchell Havemeyer steps between me and the shelf. He says, 'Not here. The books on whale fishery that you'll want to see are in the back room. Come.'

He spreads the yellow flowery curtain to let me enter the back room. There's a large pine table in the centre of the room, four chairs, and wood and glass bookcases covering all the walls. Above them are framed pictures of enormous whales and of all kinds of whaling ships. Master Henry Mitchell Havemeyer invites me to have a seat. He stands over me smiling. He gestures towards the wood and glass cases and says, 'It's at your disposal. Where do you wish to begin?' His shoulders shake with mirth. He says, 'I'm a terrible host! Without coffee, books are often just books. Sister Mary! Will you step in here?'

A door opens and I can't help but be astonished when I see Master Henry Mitchell Havemeyer's wife: she bears such a resemblance to Lizzie Melville – how is it possible? The same look in her eyes, the same deep centre-part separating her hair, the same long black dress closed at the neck by a gold brooch. The only way of telling it isn't Lizzie Melville is by the feet – those coming towards us are bare.

Sister Mary smiles. I say, 'I'm called Nathaniel and I'm accompanying Monsieur Melville on his last trip. It's thanks to him that I'm here – to learn about whale fishery before I board the *Acushnet*.'

She scratches at a small spot on the table with the tip of her thumb. I'm eager for her to finish and leave. Time seems to be passing very fast now that I'm in the back room. Master Henry Mitchell Havemeyer says, 'Sister Mary, I'd be much obliged if you fixed us some coffee. And bring us some hardtack. But I beg you, stop scratching at that old pine table: it doesn't set any better with it than it does with me.'

As soon as the door closes Master Henry Mitchell Havemeyer rubs his hands together, then gets up from his chair and goes to one of the bookcases; he takes a key from his pocket and rattles it in the lock. He selects several large volumes which he comes and places in front of me. He says, 'If you really are slated to leave with Monsieur Melville tonight, you'll have to know all of this.'

I open the first work. I forget Master Henry Mitchell Havemeyer and Sister Mary right away; I'm too absorbed in my reading to even notice when she brings the coffee and hardtack. Since the beginning of recorded history, it seems, the whale has fired the imagination of hunters, poets and philosophers. In antiquity it was Aristotle who made the first of a long series of studies on the Cetacea, studies that were quite often eccentric and full of tall tales. However, Aristotle himself didn't engage in the fanciful flights of his followers that the *Speculum Regale* Master Henry Mitchell Havemeyer has placed in my hands illustrates so well.

Upon reading this work, written in the Middle Ages, one sees that the whale didn't escape the Judaeo-Christian movement which, as elsewhere, bore fruit where he was concerned. It wasn't until after Christ that whales were divided

into two categories: good and bad. For Icelandic sailors there was a time when it was forbidden to pronounce the name of the 'Devil whale'. If a sailor forgot the taboo he went without food. And it is told that an Irish monk by the name of Saint Brendan, off in search of the promised land, stepped out of the boat after a long initiatory voyage onto what he took to be a moving island in the Atlantic. He set up an altar there right away and celebrated mass before realizing that he was standing on the back of a mighty whale!

I cease reading and look up at Master Henry Mitchell Havemeyer. I already know everything in his old book because of Job J's notebooks. And I believe I've read *Moby-Dick* enough times to know that Melville retained from his reading primarily what contributed to the mythology surrounding the whale – his magnificent mouth, his enormous tail, his gigantic size and Promethean blast, all magical attributes which say that the mighty whale is more than a mere mighty whale.

But I didn't come to Nantucket to penetrate the mystery. Rather I came simply to embark with Queequeg and Melville upon the *Acushnet*. What I don't yet know I'll learn during the trip. When I say this to Master Henry Mitchell Havemeyer, he nods his head, though little inclined to leave matters there. He says, 'You'll soon be sailing the seven seas, going to the farthest reaches of the Pacific. That's fine. But how do you expect to get by if you know nothing about hunting whales?' I say, 'In January, 1841, Melville knew no more than I, and it didn't stop him from leaving on the *Acushnet*.' He says, 'Doubtless. But are you even aware that the English named the Sperm Whale after the spermaceti he provides, he being the only one that does?' I say, 'Yes, I know, thanks to Job J. I even know you find it in the sinus cavities and that it was once used to make candles, and in bleaches, and especially in medicines. Magical properties were ascribed to spermaceti because it was believed to be the whale's seed, his sperm. As an ointment for the skin it seems it worked wonders.'

Master Henry Mitchell Havemeyer mops his brow. I can see he's quite unhappy now that he knows whom he's dealing with. As a Québécois I'm used to playing myself down, but there are limits! Especially now as I dream in this Nantucket back room waiting for Melville. Master Henry Mitchell Havemeyer gets up, goes to his bookcase from which he draws an enormous tome, returns and sets it in front of me. He says, 'But then do you know the real conditions under which a whale hunt takes place?'

I glance at the thick volume. Just what I feared: the book in front of me is the kind I hate – a veritable gelatinous mass of information which I'd get nothing out of even if I were to read it. I prefer to follow my own idea, being aware that before the Americans, whaling wasn't a real industry. Coastal peoples the world over hunted whales for the simple reason that whales appeared on their shores. The Biscayans made a name for themselves because they lived next to a bay which Leviathan frequented. It was by chance that the Basques, fishing for cod along the banks of Newfoundland, ran into whales and began to do on this side of the Atlantic what they had engaged in for centuries in Europe. But since they didn't know the techniques of melting down the blubber on the ship, they were forced to carry the whale upon a beach and flense it there, boiling the blubber in enormous ovens built especially for the purpose. Thus it is that on the Île-aux-Basques next to Trois-Pistoles you can still see the remains of one of their melters dating from the days when they scoured the St. Lawrence estuary.

This kind of fishing has been described by a large number of sailors, of whom John Harris is one. Master Henry Mitchell Havemeyer points to Harris' text. He says: 'See for yourself.' So I read; I'm confused at first because I think I've seen it all before in one of Job J's small black notebooks. How could he have found his way here to this back room in Nantucket? John Harris says: 'Once it is dead, the whale is hauled alongside the ship's hull. There, with large knives, its

flanks are carved into wide strips. Afterwards, flesh and blubber are peeled off and hoisted onto the ship by means of huge tackle. A number of these strips are then strung on ropes, eventually to be deposited on a beach, where, being lifted by a crane, they are hacked into smaller pieces. These are then cut into pieces no larger than a man's hand and tossed into vats. As soon as the solid matter has turned brown it is removed, leaving only the oil. The oil is then poured into a basin half-full of water to cool and cleanse it; it is next conducted by long troughs, which completes the cooling process, to barrels along the beach. During this time, the head of the whale is cut off in order to remove the baleen, which is bound in packages of fifty separate pieces. The rest of the head is then boiled to extract the remaining oil.'

I hand Master Henry Mitchell Havemeyer his book. I say, 'But that's ancient history. Don't you realize that we're in 1841 and that whaling ships are all equipped with try-

Whale-ship's oven.

works now? That simple invention changed everything; the *Acushnet*, which I'll eventually sail on with Monsieur Melville, is the ideal model of a whaler.' He says, 'Yes, but think that you're signing on for four years, and that tonight you're going to leave Nantucket and won't stop again until you reach the Azores or the Cape Verde Islands to complete the crew. They've got some mighty fine harpooneers in those places. Then you'll set out again and won't come back to Nantucket till the hold is full of oil. Aren't you somewhat apprehensive?' I say, 'Not in the least.' He says, 'Of course, you'll be with Mister Melville. But do you know what life is going to be like on board ship?' I say, 'Job J taught me all that.' He says, 'Even about the worms in the flour, the moldy meat and that awful hardtack?' I say, 'Even about that, Master Henry Mitchell Havemeyer. The whaling life holds no secrets for me.'

Though he continues to speak, I no longer listen to Master Henry Mitchell Havemeyer. My mind is on Melville, who must be in Captain Ahab's cabin discussing signing me on the *Acushnet*. I take a sip of coffee, and grimace because it doesn't taste exactly like coffee. What did Sister Mary put in it? What dark drug to sap my strength and leave me senseless? When I look at Master Henry Mitchell Havemeyer, he smiles, showing me his long white teeth. I shudder – his smile entraps me; it's too much like the tiny black man's smile at Arrowhead. I'd like to wake up, put on my hat and run to Melville; I suddenly feel cut off from him. This fear welling in me – am I to spend the rest of my days here in the stillness of this back room examining a bunch of dusty old books? But I'm riveted to my chair, fascinated; Master Henry Mitchell Havemeyer is moving around me, determined to tell me things which I'm no longer interested in now since layers of darkness are steadily settling over Nantucket. I say, 'I have to go.' He says, 'Of course. But look at this first.'

I shove the huge bound volumes aside and draw to me the one Master Henry Mitchell Havemeyer is pointing to. At first glance it doesn't look like much. But seeing the title jolts me. How did Master Henry Mitchell Havemeyer come into possession of the abbé Ferland's *Opuscules,* a book almost impossible to find even in Québec? He answers my question with loud laughter. He says, 'I got it from Patrick Paradis whose ancestors came from the Saguenay. After going to New Bedford to hunt the mighty whale, Patrick Paradis settled in Nantucket. He's been the proprietor of a luxurious hotel here for some years now. How he came by this book, I don't know. All I know is that he made me a present of it.'

I look up at Master Henry Mitchell Havemeyer but it's not him I see. Job J Jobin has come back from Mattavinie and is sitting alone at the end of the table. He's wearing his wide-brim hat and smiling at me over his pipe. I escape from my terror by sinking like a drowning man into the abbé Ferland's work.

With reason. I learn from the abbé Ferland that besides those Québécois living in inland isolation, there were others for whom the water was the great symbol of liberty – thanks to the St. Lawrence it was possible to escape from life's daily routine. The abbé Ferland knew the history of the Basques who, for centuries, had hunted whales as far as the Saguenay. In his short work he even backs up the pretensions of Job J. Jobin who traces his origins to Saint-Jean-de-Luz, principal spot of the Basque fishermen. It seems that the ancestor Jobin became a Québécois when he deserted his ship as it was foundering in the Baie des Ha-Ha. Legend has it that he was taken in by a tribe of Montagnais who made a red-man of him. Whence Champlain's astonishment when he noticed among the savages some with pale skin and blue eyes. This according to his own report. One among those he met proudly showed him an old harpoon which he still used to strike whales come to spawn in the mouth of the Saguenay. Supposedly Job J came from that Jobin. Moreover his grandfather was known as a proud fisherman who knew the St. Lawrence like the back of his hand from having spent his life

Whale-flensing on the Île aux Basques near Trois-Pistoles.

upon it. From him Job J learned all about whaling in the Québécois waters and the great importance it once had. As though in support of what the abbé Ferland says, Philip F. Purrington writes that the *Canadiens* were master harpooneers and that at Nantucket as at New Bedford they weren't unhappy where they had one among the crew. It wasn't the *Canadiens*' fault if the ranks of the large schools in the St. Lawrence grew thinner, being decimated by excessive, uncontrolled fishing. They'd have needed to build boats capable of following the whales to their new destination, to the icy northern waters as well as to the South Seas. But those in power preferred to send our best wood to England to satisfy Her Majesty's demands. Thus the Québécois found themselves beggars as before, condemned to patrol the St. Lawrence on small schooners which were unsuited for the high seas. No surprise, then, that after the Conquest whaling in the St. Lawrence Gulf and elsewhere lost its letters patent of nobility and became the meagre trade of a few indomitable sailors such as Samuel Robertson from the outpost at La Tabatière, who tried to trap whales in the strait with an enormous net. The abbé Ferland says:

'This Mr. Robertson hoped that, following his usual route, the whale would run into the net; the harpooneers were then to seize the occasion and deal a death blow to the unfortunate cetacean tangled in the folds. The fishermen were familiar with the vigorous battler with whom they were dealing; they argued that the moorings, holding down one side of the net, should be weak enough to break upon first contact; ceding thus, the nets would be less likely to break and would entangle the whale all the more surely than if the two sides were equally solid; for then the whale would stave through and continue on his way. But the counsel was too good to be taken; with the result that the first whale went straight through the net, leaving it in such a lamentable state that there was nothing to do but wordlessly collect it. After this first attempt, fishing for whales with nets was discontinued.'

But in the middle of the nineteenth century, whales were still being hunted in the St. Lawrence. The abbé Ferland, as a missionary in Labrador, was present at a fabulous catch of a Sulphur Bottom. Job J has spoken so much to me about it that it's particularly moving to read it in the *Opuscules*:

'In the course of the afternoon they came to announce that a schooner had entered the neighbouring port with an enormous whale in tow. We were invited to the flensing of it. We were so pleased with the invitation that we arrived at Captain Stewart's schooner just at the moment the men were beginning their work. The whale had been killed by Captain Coffin, who received the aid of Captain Stewart to secure it. A single thrust of the lance had sufficed to kill the whale, which belonged to those known as Sulphur Bottom, a type possessing remarkable vigour. Disporting themselves, it is not rare to see them shoot straight up out of the water. They accomplish this magnificent feat with the strength of their tail alone.

'The day following upon our visit, Captain Stewart entered into the port containing the melting-house to there deposit his charge. He had as well a baby whale in tow, in order that I might see it, found in the body of the whale; it had already grown to over fourteen feet in length.'

If in the course of my dream I remain so long upon the abbé Ferland, it's because I want Master Henry Mitchell Havemeyer to know that my equivocal country hasn't always been invisible; that for a long time it had its place in the society of nations. And then – well, I like the abbé Ferland. He didn't come all the way to Nantucket to accompany me to the *Acushnet* for nothing. He wanted to deliver the testament of the Québécois whale fishermen to me. The abbé Ferland says:

'The vessels used for hunting whales in the St. Lawrence Gulf are large, strong schooners capable of withstanding storms; for to realize a profit from this business, one must remain always at sea. Hanging at each side is a small whaleboat always ready to be lowered into the water upon signal. Each schooner's crew numbers some twenty men who must be vigorous and hearty rowers; for it happens that they must row for whole days at a time. Before, they would row directly up to the whales; today, the whales have become so defiant that the least noise puts them on their guard. Thus, when a short distance away, oars are exchanged for canoe paddles, which make little noise in the water.

'The manner of paying the sailors varies; some receive a fixed wage; others receive a portion of the profits from the hunts. Among Captain Coffin's men were pointed out to me two Micmacs from the Baie de Gaspé; both appeared to be very skilled at flensing whales. These savages make excellent sailors; there have been ships with crews composed entirely of Micmacs that were worth every bit as much as the others.'

But that was a hundred years ago, at the time when the Americans came to rob the birds' nests on the Île Bonaventure; they sold the eggs in Nantucket and New Bedford for

A young sailor's courage.

fifty cents a dozen. But that was a hundred years ago, at the time when the Americans came with clubs to kill the birds on the Île Bonaventure for their feathers; they used them to make beautiful pillow cases and fine mattresses which were famous as being the most comfortable on the continent.

But that surely has nothing to do with my dream, which sees me still in Master Henry Mitchell Havemeyer's back room, the captive of the abbé Ferland's *Opuscules* and of a cup of coffee and a few large pieces of hardtack. Aesop was right: you start out for the bath and wind up in the police station! It's understandable then that I should be in no particular hurry to look up at Master Henry Mitchell Havemeyer who, old sorcerer that he is, must have some more tricks to play on me.

I clear my throat to be able to speak. Then I raise my head. Master Henry Mitchell Havemeyer is no longer sitting in front of me; on the pine table there are only his glasses which make me think of a toad's big eyes. When I try to rise, a hand lands on my shoulder. It's Sister Mary's – or Lizzie Melville's, I'm not sure which. There is only a voice saying, 'You seemed very interested in what you were reading so Master Henry didn't dare disturb you. He's gone down to the docks for some fish. We both love chowder. Master Henry asked me to invite you for supper. Will you stay?' I say, 'I'm sorry, but I really can't. I have to go meet Monsieur Melville on the *Acushnet*. Give my apologies to Master Henry.'

I stand up and allow Sister Mary to pass in front of me so that she can open the front door of the store. On her right leg now she's wearing a large plaster cast. It reminds me of something but I can't think of what. Sister Mary offers me her hand. Then she points to her leg and says, 'I've got two silver clamps just above the knee; Jos' doings. I'll have to learn to smile again. Good luck, Mister Hawthorne.'

I rush out into the street, happy to have gotten away like this; my dream seems on the verge of petering out. But, curiously, seeing how dark it is in Nantucket gives me new strength. I take off running towards the Whaling Museum. Everything's happened so fast! It seems to me that Melville and I just left the packet boat surrounded by screeching tourists armed with cameras. What happened in the Nantucket sky? Perhaps just a big storm that has darkened everything. But despite my monkey jacket, I'm shivering; this strange cold that has settled over Nantucket is cutting right through me. Luckily the Whaling Museum isn't far from Master Henry Mitchell Havemeyer's back room! Otherwise I'd never reach it.

I push open the door and find myself in a large hall in which tourists are circling around a whaleboat readied to be lowered for the hunt. The director's office is at the back. He is standing completely still in front of his door, staring at the mizzenmast; he reminds me of one of those Egyptian statues made of sand and foam that you see now and then in Macy's window. I go up to him and say, 'Has Monsieur Melville been looking for me?' He says, 'I don't know if it was a Mister Melville or a Mister Coffin, but somebody came asking for a certain Nathaniel. He was with a weird character who was toting a harpoon – tattooed from head to foot. Are you this Nathaniel?' I say, 'I am. Where are they?' He says, 'I've no idea. They left a package for you and went out again. Wait here. I'll get it for you.'

He goes into his office and comes out again right away; he gives me a small parcel which I open on the spot, being too excited to wait until I'm outside the Whaling Museum. There is nothing in it, nothing except a pitiful whale's tooth which I brought with me from Québec for Melville to recognize me by. I say, 'Did they tell you where they were going? Didn't they leave a message?' He says, 'We don't write a lot around here. If they had left one, I'd know it. But tell me – do you like that mizzenmast? There's a faulty knot at the top. Do you see it?'

I take off running with my whale's tooth under my arm,

unable to believe what I'm thinking about Melville and Queequeg. I've got to get to the port before the whole of Nantucket is sadly iced in. There are huge fires all along the beach. How eager I am to reach them! How eager I am to see the *Acushnet* tied up at the dock waiting only for me to set sail!

An old sailor is walking back and forth along the docks. I ask him where the *Acushnet* is and he points to a ship gently gliding through the water. I look at it, unable to move. Leaning over the side are Melville and Queequeg quietly talking. They didn't wait! I have to catch up with them! I have to! Isn't tomorrow January 3, 1841?

The old sailor says, 'Take my rowboat. If you row hard enough, you'll catch them.'

I rush down to the beach and climb onto Queequeg's coffin-raft; with my whale's tooth secure, I begin to row furiously after the *Acushnet* – it's like striking the water with long swords, and this cold that has suddenly settled upon me.

□

END OF VOLUME ONE

Index

Acushnet, the 120, 141-2, 147-8, 150-1, 158, 161-2, 164, 170, 174, 177, 181, 186, 188, 190
Adam 141
Adams, John Quincy 67, 100
Adirondack Highway, the 143
Aeneid, the 20, 31
Aesop 181
Africa 124
Ahab, Captain 27-28, 124, 170, 173, 181
Albany 71-2, 75-6, 79-80, 82, 87-8, 94, 97, 100, 102, 104, 125, 143, 135, 138, 141
Albany Academy, the 97, 102
America 42-4, 63-4, 67-8, 100, 119, 123, 124, 128, 138, 144
Amsterdam 159
Antonin 164
Aristotle 174
Arrowhead 34-5, 111, 143-4, 150, 153, 181
Atlantic Ocean, the 120, 123, 159, 177-8
Azores, the 181

Baie des Ha-Ha, the 182
Baillargeon Transport 103
Banquo 136
Barlow, Joel 58
Bartleby, the Scrivener 88, 91, 104
Basques, the 182
Beauchemin, Abel 20, 54, 61, 72, 80-5, 107-18, 147
Beauchemin, Charles ('Father') 14, 17, 21, 38, 40, 42, 50, 53-4, 57, 60-3, 68, 71-2, 75-6, 78-88, 93-4, 97-100, 107-8, 111-18, 125, 129, 138, 143
Beauchemin, Gabriella 14
Beauchemin, Jos 17, 115, 116, 188
Beauchemin, Judith 38, 79, 83, 107-8, 113, 143
Beauchemin, Mathilde 82
Beauchemin, Steven 14, 17
Beaulieu Street 156
Bible, the 67, 124
Billy Budd 30, 32, 34-35, 88, 123-4, 132, 142, 154, 162
Biscayans, the 178
Blanche 113, 143, 144
Bleecker Street 63, 74-6, 156
Bolton, Harry 129-30, 132-3
Bombay 159
Boston 31, 58, 60, 64, 67, 74, 100, 156
Boston Tea Party, the 44, 47
Bougainville 151-2
Bourget, Monseigneur 120
Bouscotte 50, 54, 83
Bouvard et Pécuchet 91-2
Broadwall 104, 106
Broadway 71, 146
Broch, Herman 6-62
Byron, Lord 97-8

Canada 162
Canadiens, the 184
Cape Horn 159
Cape of Blanco 160
Carroll, Lewis 144, 172
Cereno, Benito 123, 154
Champ de Mars 120
Champlain 182
Chase, Jack 129, 135, 162
Chekhov 64
Chénier, Jean-Olivier 120
Christ 174
Claggart 132
Clarel 162
Coffin, Captain 143, 149, 185-6, 189
Coffin, Peter 160-2
Coffins, the 168
Colborne, Satan 120
Communipaw 141
Confidence Man, The 48
Connecticut 64
Conquest, the 184
Cook, Captain 22, 151-2
Cortland Street 76

Daggoo 125
Daytona Beach 143
Death of Virgil, the 20, 61
Denmark 123
Devil whale 177
De Wolf, John 87, 97-104, 126, 133
Divine Comedy, the 20
Doctor Sax 156
Don Quixote 20, 108
Doris, the 144
Dublin 31, 128, 159

Eden 141
Encylopedists, the 67
England 119, 123, 129-30, 152-3, 169, 184
Europe 64, 178

Fairhaven 142
Ferland, the abbé 182, 184-6, 188
Ferron, Jacques 63
Finnegans Wake 14, 20
Flatheads, the 168
Flaubert, Achille-Cléophas 57-8
Flaubert, Gustave 57-8
Florida 38, 113
Fort Stanwix 43, 47
France 47, 58, 72
Frédérick, Pierre 43, 138
French Revolution, the 58
Friponne, Ruelle de la 103

Gaddis, Mrs. 103
Gansevoort, Maria 43, 47
Gansevoort, Peter 94, 97-100, 102, 104, 135-6, 141
Gansevoort Village 43
Gansevoorts, the 43-4, 67-8, 79, 94, 100, 102
Gaspé 113, 148-9
Gaspé, Bay of 186
Gespeg 113
Gilliat 20
Girod 120
Glamis 136
Golem of Prague 154
Grande Tribu, la 14, 22
Great Britain 125, 129
Greeks, the 125
Greenbush 135, 138
Greenwich Village 63

Halifax 159
Harlem 27-8, 30, 149, 152, 155, 162
Harris, John 178
Hawthorne, Nathaniel 22, 38, 64, 132, 152-5, 162, 164, 188
Henlett 67
Hochelaga 120
Holland 123
Honolulu 106

Hudson River 43
Hugo, Victor 21, 27-8, 31, 107
Hussey, Joshua 172
Husseys, the 168

Idiot de la famille, l' 57
Île Bonaventure 186, 188
178, 182
Île-aux-Basques 178, 182
Iliad, the 18
Illinois 60
Immaculate Conception 50, 54
Immaculate Consumption 50, 54
Ireland 123
Irving, Washington 138
Ishmael 35, 112

Jackson, Andrew 44, 47, 63, 67-8, 100
Java Sea, the 160
Jobin, France 14, 111-3, 118, 159
Jobin, Job J 14, 112-4, 118, 177-8, 181-5
Joyce, James 31, 79

Kansas 168
Kaufmann, Julien 38, 113, 143
Kerouac, Jack 21, 108, 112, 156
Kidd, Captain 97-9, 102, 141
Kotzebue 152

Labrador 185
Lady Macbeth 136
Lansingburgh 88, 133
La Pérouse 152
Leviathan 178
Liffey, the 128
Liverpool 72, 106, 119, 123, 125-6, 128-9, 132-3
London 72, 119, 130
Long Ghost 129
Longue-Pointe 17, 120
Lord Lovely 130

Louis XIV 60
Lowry 128
Lowry, little girl-student 137

Macbeth 135, 136-7, 141
Macy's 189
Madagascar 128
Madame Bovary 88, 90-1
Malcolm 137
Manhattan 146
Mapple, Father 97
Market Street 102
Massachusetts 24, 133, 168
Mattavinie 112-5, 118, 133, 159, 182
Max the Dutchman 123
Melville, Allan 43, 47, 50, 60, 63, 68, 71-2, 79-80, 87, 91, 94, 97
Melville, Allan, Jr. 47, 58
Melville, Augusta 47, 68, 71-2, 74, 76, 94, 97-9, 102, 126, 128, 133-6, 138, 141, 151
Melville, Fanny 47, 152
Melville, Gansevoort 47, 88
Melville, Helen Maria 47
Melville, Kate 47
Melville, Lizzie (Elizabeth Shaw) 24, 28, 34-5, 94, 120, 148-53, 173-4, 188
Melville, Malcolm 27-8, 30, 32, 34, 36, 87-8, 129, 151, 162
Melville, Maria 63, 72, 87, 100
Melville Museum, the 144
Melville, Thomas (Major) 44, 58, 60, 74, 156
Melville, Thomas, IV 47, 58-60, 71, 104
Miami, the 168
Micmacs, the 186
Middle West, the 174
Missouri (state of) 168
Mitchell's Book Corner 172
Mitchell-Havemeyer, Master Henry 170-82, 186-9

195

Mitchell-Havemeyer, Sister
    Mary 173-4, 188
Moby-Dick 20, 27, 30, 32, 34, 38,
    48, 50, 63, 67, 79, 88, 91, 93,
    102, 108, 112, 114, 120, 125,
    142, 159, 167, 177
Mohawks, the 168
Monroe, James 58
Montagnais, the 115, 163, 182
Montréal 119-120, 148
Montréal-Nord 80, 103

Nantucket 150, 158-9, 162, 167-
    70, 172, 177-8, 181-2, 184, 186,
    189-90
Negro slaves 125
Nepos, Captain 152
New Bedford 141, 150-1, 154-6,
    158-9, 170, 173, 182, 184, 186
New England 119, 167
New World, the 130
New York 24, 36, 43-4, 58, 64,
    67, 76, 79-80, 94, 99-100, 102,
    104, 119, 125, 129, 132, 141,
    146, 150, 155-6, 159-60, 169
New York Times, the 36
Noah 116

Omoo 50
Opuscules 182, 185, 188

Pacific Ocean, the 67, 132, 177
Paradis, Patrick 182
Paris 28, 58
Pearl Street 43
Pequod, the 125
Pernety, Dom 64
Pierre or the Ambiguities 48, 50,
    88, 94
Pitkins, the 64
Pittsfield 143, 146, 152, 154, 172
Pluto (the black man) 41, 138
Poe, Edgar Allan 138
Pointe-Bleue 115, 163

Potomac, the 156
Purrington, Philip F. 184
Pyramids of Egypt, the 119

Quakers, the 169
Québec 20, 148, 162, 182, 189
Québécois, the 178, 182, 184, 186
Queen of England, the 129
Queequeg 35, 112, 125, 129, 132,
    162-4, 167, 170, 177, 190

Récamier, Madame 58
Recherches philosophiques sur les
    Américains 64
Recognitions, The 20
Redburn 87, 102-3, 128-32
Redburn, Wellingborough 129,
    130
Red Coats, the 120
Riga, Captain 123
Rivière-des-Prairies, city of 103
Robertson, Samuel 184
Robinson Crusoe 138
Rokovoko 170
Rosemont 103
Rousseau, Jean-Jacques 67
Rue St-Denis 164

Sacré-Coeur Hospital 108
Saguenay, the 182
Saint Brendan 177
Saint-Eustache 120
Saint-Jean-de-Dieu 81, 84, 113
Saint-Jean-de-Luz 182
St. Lawrence, the 119-30, 151
St. Lawrence Estuary 178
St. Lawrence Gulf 148, 184, 186
St. Lawrence River 120, 182,
    184-5
Saint-Michel, city of 103
Samm 112-19
Saratoga 43
Sartre, Jean-Paul 28, 32, 57-58,
    68, 79, 88, 90-1

Savages, the 64, 71-2, 125
Scotland 44
Scott 67
Seattle 31
Shakespeare, William 135-8, 141
Shaw, Elizabeth *see* Melville, Lizzie
Sikes District 135, 137-8, 141
South Seas, the 141, 151-2, 162, 167, 173, 184
Speculum Regale, the 174
Spermaceti 177
Sperm Whale, the 177
Spouter's Inn, the 147, 159
Starbuck 169
Stavrogin 116
Stewart, Captain 185-6
Stuart, Gilbert 43
Sturgeon, Abraham 146
Sulphur Bottom 144, 149, 185
Swain, Nathan 160

Tabatière, La 184
Tahiti 106
Tashtego 125, 168, 170
Tomkins, Governor 103

Toilers of the Sea 27
Torquemada 124
Trois-Pistoles 81, 84
Two Years Before the Mast 138
Typee 106

Ulysses 20
Una 17, 113, 118
United States of America, the 151

Vancouver 151
Vanderscamp, Yan Yost 138, 141
Vere, Captain 123
Versailles 60
Virgil 20, 31, 61
Virginia, Council of 64

Walcotts, the 64
Wall Street 100
Washington, city of 31, 44, 67
Washington, George 43, 125
Whale Museum, the 170, 172, 189
White House, the 67
Whitman, Walt 22
Wild Goose Tavern, the 141
Winkle, Rip Van 138

Editor for the Press: Frank Davey
Typeset in Stempel Garamond
and printed in Canada

For a list of other books
write for our catalogue
or call us at (416) 979-2217

THE COACH HOUSE PRESS
401 (rear) Huron Street
Toronto, Canada M5S 2G5